Grifton, a Novel

Roland Mullins

Old Seventy Creek Press 2018

GRIFTON, a Novel

Old Seventy Creek Press 2018

TO DAD, MOM & THE FAMILY

Lloyd Aden Mullins (1894-1962) Hattie Roosevelt Morris Mullins (1900-1986), Roland Dyche (Jenna Phillips) Mullins, Carrie Mullins (Bobby Lynn Amburgey), Callie Mullins Shaffer (Mikhael) & youngest grandchild Carolina Mullins

Published in the United States by:
Old Seventy Creel Press
Rudy Thomas, Editor & Publisher
P. O. Box 204
Albany, Kentucky 42602

ISBN-13: 978-0-9982374-5-9
ISBN-10: 0-9982374-5-0

ACKNOWLEGEMENTS

Thanks to Dr. Henry Borne, James Broaddus, Sir Roger Coldiron, Martha Cox, Nancy Mullins, and Dr. Callie Shaffer for reading and providing helpful comments on the manuscript. The gracious computer/printing assistance provided by the Honorable Bobby L. Amburgey, and the Honorable Carrie C. Mullins made finalizing the work possible. To Rudy Thomas and Old Seventy Creek Press for the excellent production, advising, and publishing, thanks.

List of Characters :

Committed to a promise he made to Grifton Davis, Caleb Grant is sorting through Grifton's life trying to compose a report about Grifton to be presented to his now grown sons. "Tell my boys about me," is haunting Caleb, the task an obsession, nearly twenty years later.

———————

Various descriptive versions of Grifton emerge:

Peachy, Grifton's step-daughter writing about him: "A slippery, absent, showman, you talked about building Mom's dream house. It was your dream house. 'Take off your shoes inside. Don't use the jacuzzi. I'm nailing your window shut.' We got the message. In a way it was a beautiful house of horrors. You spent a lifetime scratching, trying to fill the dirty, dark hollow from your past."

———————

Poppa said, "Grifton is a hero to hear people talk. Never worked a day in his life. Gambles they say. Glitter comes from the trunk of that car—plumb full of watches, gold, diamonds, necklaces, heirloom stuff. It's funny to me how the sorrier you are the more people talk about you—even after you die."

———————

Crit Rose, the gambler crime boss, describes Grifton: "He was the character of the group, the man to beat, too. He had the fastest hands I ever saw. We all knew he cheated but no one ever figured out how. Bell County once said,

'Grifton could make a deck of cards dance a waltz.' Grifton was the most interesting man I ever met. Seemed to be able to read people's minds."

Forrest, Grifton's son reports, "He was my best friend."

Del, Peachy's brother remembers: "Grifton sent money to two children's organizations—hundreds of dollars."

W. H., the old defense attorney had his own take on Grifton. "Quite a mix up. Two boys brought before the court, nearly the same age, sired by that scoundrel in his old days. Two mothers, and the old codger married to neither."

Cover Art by Rosemary Mathieu

TABLE OF CONTENTS

INTRODUCTION 9
GRIFTON SEARCH & RAILERY AT THE MCDONALDS 14
WILLIAM HARRISON SEEKING TRUTH & JUSTICE 19
BURN THE SCHOOL 24
CICERO SPEAKS 29
INCARCERATION 34
GAMBLING FRIENDS 38
SCAM 44
GRIFTON'S NEIGHBOR 51
THE OBSESSION 56
LOCATING THE BOYS 62
FRED WRINKLER EVANGILIZING 67
GEORGIA BELL "PEACHY" DAVIS 73
PEACHY & DELL, SOMETHING BIG 80
DELL ESCAPES 85
KNOT HEAD'S INFORMATION 90
FINDING DEL 97
ACE & DUCE 103
ROBERT LEE "DUCE" 107
HAVING GRIFTON'S THOUGHTS 110
GRIFTON GOES DEEP 112
AMOS MOON NEEDS HELP 119
ACE & DUCE TELL THEIR TALES 124
FORREST HAS ANOTHER PEACHY CONNECTION 129
THE RESTART 137
GRIFTON'S REDEMPTION 144
UNEXPECTED QUEST 148
THE BOAT RECLAIMED 153
FROM DICUSSIONS WITH MANDY 157
PERSONAL THOUGHTS FOR THE DAVIS REPORT 160
ULYSSES ASSISTS 163
PARSING THE FIND 172
GRIFTON RESURRECTED 173
HOME AGAIN WITH AFTER THOUGHTS 178
PERSONAL CONCLUSION 181

NOTES: 182

ABOUT THE AUTHOR 183

INTRODUCTION

"It's funny to me how the sorrier you are the more people talk about you—even after you die." I didn't know if Poppa was talking just to be talking or getting ready to teach me something. He often did both. We were traveling south on highway 290 just out of town. He was letting me listen to rock and roll music on the truck radio.

I was weaving and bobbing to *Stagger Lee cried Billy, I'm gonna let you go at that, you've done won all my money and my brand-new Stetson Hat."* So, I wasn't sure if he was going to lecture me about bobbing and weaving or the behavior of Stagger Lee.

"Hum," I said.

Poppa continued, "You see that car back there in the curve? Navy blue Cadillac, trunk open."

"No," I said.

"Anyway," Poppa said, "that was Grifton Davis." After Poppa's introduction, I did remember seeing him, leaning against the front door of the car, tall, lean, white shirt untucked, black slacks. "That guy gets more play than Stagger Lee or All Shook Up." I didn't know Poppa even knew those two songs but was pleased that he did. "Grifton is a hero to hear people talk. Never worked a day in his life. Gambles supposedly. Glitter comes from the trunk of that car—plumb full of watches, gold necklaces, diamonds, heirloom stuff. Good quality too. Ever woman in the county is looking for him, never asking where the goods come from—priced way below wholesale, you see."

I think I was thirteen when I saw the Cadillac with Poppa. That's the last time I saw Grifton, at least until I was well past sixteen. A group of us boys had stopped at a roadside so-called restaurant. I didn't hear any grease popping or see anybody eating. The proprietor sat at the only table smoking Lucky Strikes, the pack visible lying by his empty coffee cup. A counter extended across one end of the room.

Grifton had an army blanket spread across a section of it and was tossing dice and watching us boys out of the corner of his eye which was black like his wavy hair. We had stopped to buy a half-pint of moonshine, to be shared four ways—just the right amount to give the inexperienced a buzz and wear off before we went home. Grifton invited us to gather around. He wanted to show us something. First, he drew from his pocket a huge, or at least it was huge to us, roll of bills with a rubber band around it. "That men," he called us men, "is 5k. I can get my coat and show you more." I thought, huh-oh he's planning to win what little money we've got. That didn't come up though. Grifton picked up the dice and tossed them on the blanket several times telling us what numbers would come up next. Then he opened his long slender hand revealing a second set of loaded dice that we had no idea was there, and I doubted that anyone else playing with him could have detected.

Encounters with Grifton were spaced. It was after a high school basketball game sometime after my truck ride with Poppa, and the dice demonstration. A wet snow had fallen, and the roads were extremely slick. My special girlfriend, Mandy, and I were traveling home from the game when a car stalled at the front of the line and Poppa's old truck slid out of control and into the back of the last car. The driver and I got out to assess the damage and Grifton rolled out of the back seat of the damaged car holding his back and moaning. The driver yelled at him. "Don't start that crap, Grifton!" I never knew why the driver addressed him so strongly, maybe because he knew I didn't have any money, or he could have remembered my brother pulling some of his family members from a fiery crash some years earlier. No more was heard about Grifton's physical complaint; however, the driver got another car at my expense. That was hard for a teenager working part-time for considerably less than a dollar an hour. The replacement car was road worn and autos were a lot cheaper in those days. Also, my brother helped me.

It was thirty years later, on arriving at the office from a lunch break, my secretary presented me a business card. The gentleman wanted me to call him. The fancy card boasted: *dealer in antiques, diamonds, gold, and heirloom pieces,* GRIFTON DAVIS. So much gossip had circulated about Grifton that I had little interest in talking to him— gambler, contacts in Las Vegas, insurance fraud, cocaine dealer, suspect in wife's murder, built most expensive houseboat on the lake, no known occupation. The list goes on.

After a couple of days my curiosity took control, and I called. He called me Grant, my last name only. "Grant, I want you to have my houseboat." Not knowing where this came from or what it meant, I ask a few questions. Unbeknownst to me he had tried to sell the boat to several towns-people. "Come out and let me show it to you." The boat was moored a few miles from my house which is on the same body of water but several road miles away. Turns out the houseboat was not a boat, in my mind it qualified as a yacht, all sixty-five feet of it. He'd had it built to his specifications. I'd never seen anything quite like it even in brochures or magazines. I had no intention of buying, but it caught my eye. Grifton had maybe a sixth-grade education, but he had a building/decorating ability far beyond the expected. In his own way, he was brilliant, had the hands of a surgeon, the tongue of a Wall Street stock salesman, and the ability to communicate messages without saying anything. He greeted me at the door looking at my shoes. He was in his sock feet.

"Your shoes aren't dirty. Come on in." Obviously, this meant, pull your shoes off—which I did. Just inside the door he addressed me by my last name again. "Grant, I want you to have this boat. I have never seen your hands dirty." Being a farmer on the side, I knew he was sugaring me, but something about it registered. I laughed and shook my head. The visit progressed to the living room-bar-kitchen area. A huge Bible was displayed on an ornate coffee table, open and ready to be read. In subsequent years when I questioned him about his salvation, he shrugged it off with, "It's too late for me".

After walking through the rooms, noting the decorative cornices, the solid cherry cabinets, the plush white carpets, the complete kitchen, the gold plumbing fixtures, the hot tub top-side, the master bedroom with the raised king size bed with two TV's—a his and hers, mounted over the foot with headphones for private viewing. My head was turned. The super salesman had bagged one. He wanted cash, as in greenbacks. Along with not knowing he'd tried to sell the boat to several people, I wasn't aware that he was under indictment in federal court for insurance fraud. Federal penitentiary was just months away. Three of his children would go along. The case was reputed to be the largest insurance fraud of its kind ever reported. Several of his associates were implicated.

Properties could be confiscated, greenbacks hidden. Proof of purchase was one consideration on my part. Further, a bank withdrawal of that amount in cash, I thought, required some kind of federal reporting. I had nothing to hide. Yet the idea left me feeling uncomfortable. I let him know that I had to maintain a proof of purchase and that we'd better deal by check. He threw his hands out to the side and said, "okay."

A close acquaintance reported having seen Grifton lift a throw rug to reveal a hundred thousand dollars in cash stashed in his bedroom, under the feet of all who entered. Cash business seemed normal to him.

I ran into Grifton next when getting gas at the local Chevron station. Men gathered there to smoke and talk most mornings. This was probably six or seven years after the boat purchase. Grifton had served his term in prison where inmates described him as knowing everyone and being listened to by most. He moved up to the level of chief in-mate cook, a good place to make friends. He supposedly lost everything in the earlier court proceedings, but on this day, he was driving a new car, and wearing a hat. The car was a Chevy instead of a Cadillac, but the hat was quality. Calling me by my last name, as usual: "Grant, I want you to do something for me." He produced from his wallet pictures of two preteen boys. "These are my boys." They were virtually the same age, and very handsome, born to different women neither of whom was Grifton's wife. "I want you to promise me that you'll tell my boys about me" was his next statement. I said, "I can try, I guess," but probably looked a bit taken back. "Tell them what good houses I built. You know what to say." I left the station with this semi-binding agreement in my head, and never saw Grifton again.

This, readers, is a sampling of the back story—now what to tell the boys.

GRIFTON DAVIS SEARCH &
RAILERY AT THE MCDONALDS

I think it was the day of the big eclipse of '17. Small planes had lined up for flight from Oregon to Carolina following the sun's path, passengers hoping to get the award-winning photo shot. Physicists moved to special locations across the globe, kindergarteners fidgeted, packing their special glasses as mothers readied them for school and a promised viewing. With all the press accounts, I wasn't likely to forget the day.

An earlier eclipse story came to mind from my family's oral history as I sat awaiting my food and daydreaming at the local McDonalds. My great-great Uncle Biggy was working in the corn field with his workhands. Suddenly the sky turned dark with not a cloud in sight. They had no forewarning. They all leaned on their hoe handles, shading their eyes with cupped hands, more than one trembled. Old Uncle Biggy yelled loudly, authoritatively. "Keep your eyes on that main figerment, boys! If it goes, out we're all gone to hell!" My memory state ended abruptly as Elmer Sigmon bumped my table in passing, so I can't speculate as to how the old timers faired without special glasses.

Elmer assumed his usual swagger as he strolled toward a table filled with fellow "club" members. He'd no doubt noted their cars parked outside, most of them not exactly between the lines. His swagger was somewhat halting after seventy-five years use.

"Hi'dy boys. All's well I hope." But Elmer saw that wasn't the case. Fred Winkler was stopped in mid-sentence, one hand on his coffee cup, the other fanning the air, not in a frantic way, but in a listen-to-me-way.

His wife, Ethel, he said, had gone into the church sanctuary the past Sunday. She had paced back and forth across the room in front of where the sacrament table should have been. She had peered at the spot where the pulpit had been.

Her eyes narrowed, her brow had furrowed, and her lower lip had drooped. "That Southern Theological School, school my foot, ruination of our preacher," she said out loud.

Fred stopped his story at this point and scanned the table to assess interest—a mistake. For Amos Moon, leaning in, captured most of the table as he announced that the recent election was about to change things.

"Don't mention election, Amos! We've wore that out." Knot Head blurted this out loud enough to cause various coffee drinkers to jump, and coffee cups to spill over. Amos, holding his position, plowed on.

"I think I told you about my woman leaving at three in the morning the day after the election, went to her mammy's." Amos stopped for breath, and Knot Head, forgetting his previous admonition, again took control.

"I'll bettcha there won't be no 'baccer' raised around here next year. This new man is going to get rid of all the Mexicans, send them back where they come from."

William Harrison, local defense attorney, appeared and ambled back to the table just in time to hear Knot Head's proclamation and to halt the discussion. W. H. waddled around the table and thumped down in a chair next to Knot Head.

"Morning gentlemen." W. H. straightened his tie and brushed at it, attacking part of some past meal. "Men when you peel us all down, we're the same yesterday, today, and tomorrow, including of course the politicians." W. H. had jumped right into the conversation without preamble. "I'm guessing that ever since man stood, looked in the four directions and determined he had a right to know and to be that our course has been set. Oh, technology changes. Knowledge increases—actually, just our vocabulary increases, but we remain the same. We're always trying to feel better, trying to better understand our creator, trying to improve our leaders. Losers say, this is the end, winners say this is the beginning."

Each of the men glanced around the table and then back at W. H. They considered W. H. an old windbag, but they had a certain respect for his learning so they listened. Among themselves though they referred to him as "Old First Responder" because he was usually first to local auto accidents.

"Remember men, this revolution we recently went through is merely a continuation." Men shuffled in their chairs, two left the table for coffee refills. They had heard W. H's revolution story before. "It has gone on every four years for over two centuries. Each side is trying to be the big dog. Just relax, enjoy your breakfast." W. H. leaned back in his chair and laced his fingers across his ponderous midsection. "You know, Amos, Plato would tell your charming wife to take up what she is good at—cooking, caring for grandchildren. Be happy. Dr. Freud on the other hand would likely suggest three-hour sessions once weekly for three or four months to get to the bottom of her neuroses." W. H. was just getting started. Knot Head didn't know how much longer he could stay.

At this point I tuned out and looked out the window studying the passing vehicles. I was on the lookout for Forrest Davis, Grifton's son. He might use the drive through. I wasn't there to eves-drop on the elderly breakfast bunch. It was inevitable, however, as they sat directly across from my table, talking to be heard by older ears. Toyota's, minivans, Fords, a double cab work truck filled with serious looking men, or maybe tired men, in hardhats were all circling to the drive- through. I was there hoping to catch Forrest who is several years older than the boys whom Grifton had requested that I tell about him. I knew Forrest frequented the restaurant on Saturday mornings. I had talked with him twice, catching him at home on his front porch on my evening walks.

Nearly a month had passed since our last talk. Phone calls and watching his porch had been futile. Forrest, during our last encounter, had reported that his dad was his best friend. He had traveled with him to Georgia to haul shinny green watermelons to grocers in several counties. They had hauled stoker coal out of the mountains during winter. "Dad had three trucks. He worked hard." That message didn't fit with local Grifton stories—never worked, gambled, sold diamonds, possible murderer, incarcerated. But another comment during our last conversation had pricked my interest.

Forrest may have observed a working father, but he also reported on a move. Grifton had moved the family several counties away when Forrest was a young boy. They remained there until his teen years. The reason for the move was to enroll Forrest's sister in a special school for advanced training.

According to Forrest, Grifton's education ended after third grade rather than sixth grade as I first guessed. So, this educational concern for the daughter, this sensitivity wasn't part of his personality picture. Previous stories told of nothing but wrong doing—now this new revelation. Could there be gray areas? There was apparently more than one side to Grifton. At this point, all I could do was complete a sketchy social history. Then maybe Grifton would begin to talk, talk revealing who he really was.

In our discussions, Forrest had talked about his family. Seven brothers and sisters were accounted for, but on second thought, Forrest had remembered more, and talked about more, not counting the two youngsters. Some were step-siblings. Three others, in their forties, had introduced themselves to me a few years earlier as Grifton's offspring. Forrest seemed to have no knowledge of these. At age sixty, one would think he'd have known about the entire family—mysterious, I thought.

The raillery at the next table ended as the crew shuffled ahead of me toward the exit. However, one tidbit was overheard just as the table emptied. Fred Winkler hadn't got to finish his story, and old deacon that he was, he felt something religious should be said. Taking hold of W. H.'s sleeve, he pulled him close and ask how his church service was the past Sunday.

"Fine, fine, Fred. We had a hell of a service, Sunday." Fred shook his head and grimaced as he headed toward the door. W. H. chuckled and limped after him.

Forrest, easily recognized by his black eyes and wavy hair, but fleshier than his dad, hadn't shown. As I got in my truck, I was again thinking about trying to catch Forrest on his front porch.

WILLIAM HARRISON
SEEKING TRUTH AND JUSTICE

Sometimes it is difficult to distinguish between being nosey and being inquisitive. I'm pretty sure my visit to the courthouse started out being inquisitive. Seeking court records on the Grifton Davis insurance fraud case pretty much falls under inquisitive—research to draw as accurate picture of Grifton as possible. "Mam, I'm here seeking your assistance." I said meekly, knowing the power that comes with a large desk and a picture of the governor hanging nearby.

"Yes, how may I be of assistance. Always glad to oblige my friends." I didn't know her and she didn't know me so there was no question, this greeting was officer speaking to a voter.

"Mam, I'm from out of town and was told to come to the circuit clerk's office for information on court cases." The clerk's office is only fifteen miles from home but in another county.

The clerk opened her desk and rummaged. Finally retrieving an emery-board, she began raking it across the nails of her right hand. Without looking away from her finger work, she responded, "What specifically are you looking for, sir?" Obviously, my being from out of town significantly reduced her attention.

"Sometime back Grifton Davis had an insurance fraud case," I said.

Without looking up, she interrupted me in midsentence, "State or federal?"

I didn't know for sure and hardly knew how to answer. I just said, "I don't know." The clerk squirmed in her seat adjusted her posture, while tugging at her skirt which had crept higher during her search for the nail instrument.

"Well, it looks like you people would know what you want before coming into a busy office." With that she rubbed her nose with the back of her hand, the one with the freshly filed nails, then felt her hair in a couple of places, and turned to the computer screen on her desk. "What did you say the name was?"

"Davis, Grifton. Grifton Davis," I said in my most officious voice.

After a few clicks, she said over her shoulder; "must be federal, we don't handle those," then continued clicking. I slunk out.

Three doors down, the circuit courtroom door was open, guarded by a hefty deputy slouched against the door frame, looking at his cell phone. I could see past him to the front where the judge sat in his black robe. The stenographer on a lower level in front of him was engaged entering every word said on an undersized, mysterious writer. Limping across the room in front of the judge's bench was William Harrison (W.H.), his left hand in his suit coat pocket, his right clamped to his coat lapel. The deputy barely made room for me to squeeze through the door and pointed to a seat in the back all the time giving attention to the phone.

"Judge, I am putting together a package of irrefutable proof of the innocence of this boy. It will allow young Davis to walk among his school chums, head held high, to hug his dear mother with no guile in his heart. I merely need a few days to organize the document in a manner that you can understand."

"Ahem, yes, Counselor, I'd appreciated being able to understand your presentation. You have two days." With that the judge brought down his gavel and announced, "Court adjourned," looking somber, and judicial, first at W. H., then at the court spectators.

W. H. managed his ponderous frame between benches along the aisle, waving at the court spectators, smiling around an unlit cigar clenched and bulging his cheek. I slipped from my bench and fell in behind him. Once out in the main hallway, I tapped his arm for attention. Turning he removed the cigar and reached for my hand, always eager to shake and talk.

"Caleb, isn't it?" he said. "I saw you at the McDonalds recently. Didn't get to speak, however, important client business had my attention." I said that was alright, I understood, and could we have a word about something.

"Yes, yes, always glad to talk with a friend." He led the way out the front door, picking up his pocket knife and various other items checked at the security entrance. I had had nothing to check and passed on through. I ask if we could have coffee, to which he readily agreed.

At the corner café, I got right to the point. "I stopped in the court just wasting time but when I saw you before the bench, I wanted to listen."

"Oh yes, yes indeed, the courtroom is an intriguing place. The mangled truths and lies of mankind's making are being plucked and weighed one by one by men of special training and commitment."

I nodded agreement and proceeded to inquire about his case. "I heard you mention your client's name, Davis, to the judge. A youngster."

"Ahem, yes, yes, guilty as sin, but you know my oath 'provide the best defense to all', live by that you know. Court appointed me. No matter, he'll get the best I've got."

"Would the boy be Grifton Davis' son?"

"Indeed, he is. Quiet a mix up too, two boys brought before the court for starting the fire over at the Christian Academy. Two different mothers, boys of nearly the same age, sired by that scoundrel in his old days." W. H. looked intently at me across his coffee cup. "Your daddy was Shelby Grant, right?"

"No, I said, that was my great uncle. My dad was Sherd."

"Oh, yes, yes, I remember. Now, your great-great grandpa was at Shiloh." I didn't wish to spend the time discussing genealogy, but W. H.'s personality controlled most of his encounters, always tipping toward his doing the talking, so I settled back and allowed him to bring the talk back to the present.

"What exactly did the boys do," I finally inquired.

"Why hellfire, they burned the guts out of several classrooms over at that Christian school. Motive? I have no idea. Thrill though, I'm guessing. You know, Caleb, we are taught that nearly every behavior is nurture in origin. I am here to tell you, the closer I look at Grifton's family, the more I'm convinced it's blood—genes that causes their downfall. You know the Good Book speaks to the passing on of sins down to the fourth generation. Of course, it's not for me to judge such things." I had somewhat the same thought regarding genes, but neither of us harbored it as fact. We both knew that children are reared much the same as their parents were reared. The behavioral cycle in these cases ducking and weaving through generations is difficult to break.

W. H. removed his glasses and leaned over the table, closer to me as though he was about to reveal something very important, a secret, "Something interesting happened a few years ago, if I might digress." Knowing W. H. was going to digress no matter what I said, I just smiled and nodded. He continued, "You may remember the young Davis man who was raised up in Laurel County, I believe, but had close ties here at home. He was Grifton's nephew. Brilliant, brilliant young man, cousin to the other nephew who went bad as a CPA, you may also remember him."

W. H. sipped his coffee, adjusted his glasses and proceeded. "I had a case of some import over in one of the mountain counties, Booneville, Hindman, I forget which county seat. Anyway, the day was most miserable, had a bout with gout, and it was flaming. After facing the judge, the jury, and other personages all day, I was virtually powerless to set one foot in front of the other and immediately sought medical attention on leaving the courtroom.

"As chance would have it, I stumbled into young Dr. Davis' office. Most cordial young man. Very knowing. Extremely accommodating. Got good treatment too." W. H. tapped his right foot on the terrazzo floor as if to show how good the treatment was. He moved on, "It wasn't a year later I read in the Lexington paper that young Dr. Davis was sentenced to prison for prescribing opioids, with both hands, you might say. There he was, a thriving practice, in a medically underserved county where he was further compensated by the government loan forgiveness program. No doubt making money by the basketful. Now beat that." W. H. paused for a response. I shook my head while putting on my most serious face. "W. H. can you give me the specifics of the charges against your current young client?"

"Yes, yes indeed. Pardon the lengthy aside. The little scamps got into the school by a window left unlatched by one of them, of course. The building's side-view camera captured the entire action. Once inside, a second camera showed them first entering the fifth-grade classroom, then fifteen minutes later the eighth-grade classroom, then a third camera pictured their entrance to the school library where the fire reportedly started." W. H. was drawing the school schematic with his finger on the table as he talked. "Police reports reveal that they turned the furniture upside down, piled the folders, books, anything that would burn out in the middle of the floor, then proceeded down the hall room to room. Little heathens. What else could you expect out of an old ass like Grifton?

"Say, Caleb, you know not to discuss or publish this discussion. Highly unethical, you understand. I certainly would never breach such a trust with just anybody. Because of the boy's tender ages, the court documents will likely be sealed."

With that, W. H. extended his hand and gave me an intense stare. I assured him, "I will take the information locked in my head to my grave."

BURN THE SCHOOL

Oftentimes reports that we receive are products of shared memories, screened through prejudices of the reporter. The end-product may be pure fiction. W. H.'s report on the Davis boys didn't appear fictional, however. His was put together from the tangle of known facts, pieced by one man trained in the art. The boys, he concluded, were "guilty as sin". A live video supported this. Police reports substantiated it. Additional information on the event requires some conjecture, that is, the actual carrying out of the deed, what was said, and the boy's actions following the burning of the school.

Literature portrays civilization as a thin fabric, easily torn, destroyed by fire, natural disaster, war. It might also be portrayed as a great taproot firmly binding the basic institutions together and feeding the order—family, religion, education, for example. The Davis boys began life in a troubled family. Their lives were broken from the beginning; the natural and universal laws given to man by his creator left unnurtured. Two layers—family and religion—of the boy's taproot are peeled back very early to dry out and die. Burning of the school may be the symbolic destruction of that which contains man's collective knowledge of where he is, who he is, where he has been, and where he seems to be going. Thus, a third layer of the taproot—education/socialization—Is now under attack.

"Wonder what old Preach will say about this," Ace was speaking loud seeking a response from Duce. I hesitate to use these two names, but they are all I have for the Davis boys. Grifton from my personal knowledge of him would not have chosen these names. He protected his persona with the locals in his dress, in his posture, in his overall presentation. Other descriptions of his personality vary considerably, coming from individuals sharing information from the light that they have. The Ace and Duce nicknames surely came from their Mothers side, one of whom was enamored with Grifton's gambling prowess. The other boy's mother's great uncle served in WW II, the European theater. He might have brought the name back with him. "Ha, what about ugly old lady Abigale?" Duce yelled this back as he crashed a chair on the teacher's desk hoping to see splinters fly. Preach and Abigale were two of their fifth-grade teachers. Ace was busy tearing pages from a social studies book, a partial-page from the book floated down over his shoulder, portraying half a figure of Lincoln at Gettysburg, the remainder of the page yet to be removed. No doubt, their name-sake, Rebel Jeff Davis, back in nineteenth century Virginia would have been delighted to see Lincoln, the invader, ripped apart. Ace had no such idea though, as matters of historical consequence likely never occurred to him. "I'm piling these chairs and desks on papers in the middle of the room. That'll look good, won't it?" Duce was sweating and swearing by this time.

"Yeah, let me finish with these books, and I'll help you! Give them something to study, right?" Ace laughed as he made this good joke. The mayhem continued room to room for the better part of the morning. Once outside, the boys sat several yards behind the building, in tall Johnson grass, its seed heads waving all around, smoke curling above from their cigarettes. Hidden by the grass they laughed and congratulated one another on the successful caper.

"Preach ain't gonna believe that just two of his fifth graders could do all that. It'll teach him to strut in and give everbody that shitty look, I betcha that." Ace was again laughing as he boasted of the magnitude of the destruction. Preach, the fifth-grade social studies teacher and minister over at the Presbyterian Church, was a saintly old man, who took needy children into his home, visited and counseled troubled families and saw the good in everyone. He did carry his short frame marine serious and wore a face that implied a total lack of tolerance for any nonsense.

"I'm gonna go back in and burn the damn thing." Duce said this as he flipped his cigarette into the weeds.

"The hell!" Ace was excited, talking fast, raking his hand over his flattop, and stepping quickly to catch up. "That'll let everbody around here know the Davis boys rule. No more ordering us around. Get your packet out. Line up. Sit in the corner. Go to the principal's office. No sir-re-bob. We're Davises. Ha, won't be no place to line up." A few minutes later the building was full of smoke and the boys were on their way down the railroad tracks.

Duce was panting, his face streaked with sweaty soot from the fire. "Where we going?"

Without looking back, Ace replied, "To the cave, the one Dad took us to that time."

Gasping for breath, Duce managed to blow out, "Long-Field Cave"?

Long-Field Cave is about a mile east of town. The only access is to walk down the CSX railroad tracts. Adventure seeking father-son hikers, family picnickers, and Cub Scout groups visit the cave, but these trips are rare. The path from the tracks down to the cave was overgrown and hardly visible. "Come on Duce. This is the way, I'm bettin'."

Duce was a bit hesitant. "Do you think a bear might live in the cave?" While he was slightly quicker to violence, to follow a punch by kicking, tripping until his opponent was down, then to fall upon him mercilessly, he was also cautious.

"Hell, no." Ace spoke with more confidence than he felt. Bear had been seen in the area. "Even if there is we'll scare the shit out of it. Now let's go." The cave was more mouth than cave. A great hole in the side of the hill, opening into one big room with ceiling fifteen feet or so high. The large room projected maybe fifty feet into the hill. Near the back of the room the floor sloped up and over a rockfall, the fall likely caused in the nineteenth century by blasting for the nearby rail construction. "Come on back here." Ace had moved beyond the rock fall to a secluded crevice just right for the boys' camp.

Duce crept from the entrance. "Oh, hell yes. We can defend this spot", he said and began gathering together fist-size rocks. As the gloaming of the day turned to darkness, spirits darkened, too.

"What do you think our Moms are saying?" Ace became aware of their predicament as he squirmed in the dust for more comfort. "I'm hungry."

Duce, more comfortable with their surrounding now, began to show his manhood. "Mine ain't missed me. Her pills are about all she ever misses. She can kiss my ass. I'm hungry, too." Sometime later, His confidence having rebounded, Duce decided to make his way over the rockfall and see what it looked like outside. The stars, visible now, were brighter than usual, absent the light pollution of town, but it was still dark in the surrounding woods. Duce's eyes focused on a set of eyes peering from the trees. They were looking right at him, he decided, and he hurried back to Ace. "There is something out there, maybe a wildcat, or bear!" Duce was breathing fast as he reported this.

"Or maybe a fox, or coyote, or coon," Ace replied.

As darkness came on the city's volunteer fire department had completed its task, and the police department was moving toward finishing theirs. After viewing the video, officers knew who the culprits were, and they were combing the neighborhood for clues as to their whereabouts. The local radio station announced that two preteens were being sought as persons of interest. Descriptions were given: "ten to twelve years old, about five feet tall; wearing tee shirts emblazoned with the Christian Academy logo on the front, their names on the back; dark hair, one cropped and combed in a flattop, the other cut marine style."

Soon a local businessman came forth with information that two boys fitting the description were seen traveling east along the railroad tracts. The police search along each side of the tracts soon lead them to the vicinity of Long-Field Cave.

Inside the dark cave Ace was mostly thinking out loud, "Duce, do you know that tall girl in the eighth grade, Charity or something like that? I heard she does it."

Duce was more concerned with something for supper. "Does what?"

"You know." Ace was getting his thoughts organized for further discussion when a better idea came to mind, "Let's play Bat Man and Robin," that might calm Duce, he thought. "I'll be Robin."

"O. K."

"Gemini-Crickets, Batman," Ace stood straight as he said this.

"Where did you get that one?" Duce asked.

"Gemini-crickets?"

"Yeah."

"Well, I was raised in a cave, you know."

Ace was ready to present another line when a light broke the darkness within the cave. Once the officers made the decision to check inside the cave, capture was imminent. What to do with the boys was the next question. Officers eventually settled on calling in the state children's services people and turning the boys over to the county attorney.

CICERO SPEAKS

It had been a couple of months since my last discussion
with William Harrison. Forrest Davis had not been located.
I was beginning to wonder if my Grifton project would ever
come to fruition. I did learn something in the lobby of the
post office this morning. Bobby Sandusky, maintenance
man over at the courthouse, asked if I knew about W. H.
being in the hospital. Feeling somewhat obligated even
though W. H. and I had not been that close, I decided to
visit the hospital and check on him.

The local hospital, serving the small town where everybody
knows one another, where people pray for the sick at
Wednesday night prayer meetings, even those who'd just as
soon not be prayed for, is not a house of strict rules. The
elderly Saturday morning McDonalds coffee club had
decided to go over in mass and see about W. H.

Fred Winkler purposefully got a head start on the rest.
"Morning, W. H. Heard you was sick. Thought I'd better
come check on you. The rest of the boys are on their way.
How you feeling?"

"Not bad. Not bad at all. Thanks for coming, Fred, needed
somebody to talk to. Should have been released yesterday,
but the wife talked old doc Whistle Britches into keeping
me for more tests, more poking and gouging, I say. Just a
little gout, but she's convinced I may be dying. Says my
entire system is under stress something about exercise, too
much meat and potatoes, McDonalds sausage and biscuits.
You've probably heard such. Why, hellfire, my daddy lived
to be eighty-nine, ate biscuits and gravy every morning,
cornbread and milk every night, smoked five or six cigars a
day, weighed twenty or thirty pounds more than I ever
have."

The old deacon had something bearing on his mind. "W.
H., I come early 'cause there is something I want to talk to
you about, if it won't hurt your feelings."

W. H. raised up and adjusted his pillow. "Why, Fred, I can't think of a thing that you might mention that would bother me in the least. When you've handled as many divorces, faced as many lawyers, and been married thirty-five years, well sir, you've been accosted on about ever front known to man. Down in Cumberland County once a man sidled up to me in the court house men's room, called me a sissy, then winked at me. I just winked back, zipped up, washed my hands, and strolled out. No, my friend, proceed and think nothing about my personal feelings." W. H. likely made the Cumberland County report up just to put Fred at ease.

"W. H., do you know the Lord? Are you saved?" Fred was speaking low, talking faster than common, and now standing over W. H. "You being in the hospital and all, I just got to worrying about it."

W. H. folded his arms across his stomach, clasped his hands with thumbs up as though to twiddle them, and smiled. "You know, Fred, that is the most pertinent two-part interrogative ever presented to me, other than from the pulpit, of course. You are not the first man to express concern about a fellow human being's spiritual condition. John Adams once wrote to Tom Jefferson saying that surely the Lord would not let such a creation as man just disappear. That was getting at the same concern many years ago, you know.

"Fred I've given substantial thought to salvation over the years. Read a lot, too. C. S. Lewis, a noted theologian/philosopher summarized the state of man very accurately, I think." W. H. squirmed, moving side to side on the bed, apparently scratching a spot. "Lewis pinned most of our bad behavior on pride. Adam to you and me, we just can't get over our nature—me first attitude, you see. Pride starts out as a necessity. If a baby didn't cry when hungry, we might not know to give nourishment. Me first, right off. This nature grows as we development. We snatch and grab, squeezing the other fellow out. This we must overcome. We must recognize it in ourselves, admit it to the Lord, ask forgiveness for it. This I've done, my friend."

Fred looking at his hands, blurted out, "That's God's only son, Christ's teaching, too, I think."

"Right, but you fellows over at the Baptist Church seem to take it a little farther, cringing at unimportant things—my vulgar speech, for example, gutter language, not cursing mind you, just using vulgaris language, a term from the Latin, low or common speech, you understand. The prophet of old reminded us that the Lord wants us to be just, merciful, and walk humbly in the presence of the Lord. I'll have to say the latter has given me pause. It's hard for a lawyer to be humble. We like to beat the other fellow, convince the judge." W. H. chuckled.

Fred was fidgeting, trying to collect his thoughts for a response. "I's just worried. I knew you saying hell fire didn't mean anything. That's in the Bible." Fred was cut short when Amos, Elmer, and Knot Head filed through the door, caps in hand, and looking somber, maybe expecting to see their old friend in a coma or worse.

Smiles broke out all around on seeing their windy friend smiling and nodding at each one. Pleasantries were exchanged. Knot Head tried to see W. H.'s feet which were partly covered by the sheet. He wanted to be able to report what gout looked like as that is what he heard W. H.'s complaint was. Talk ranged from arrests reported in the weekly paper, the burning of the school, Trump tweets, the University of Kentucky's upcoming basketball season, and sundry other timely topics. A lull finally settled in.

Knot Head got up and walked over to the window and looked out on the hospital parking lot where he saw Fred's Baptist preacher climb from his car. "Say, Fred, you never finished telling us about Ethel's problems with the preacher over at your church. You remember that Saturday at the McDonalds."

All eyes turned to Fred hoping to break the lull and keep the visit going. W. H. was apparently enjoying the company. After taking what seemed like several minutes studying his shoes, Fred sighed and began. "I don't rightly know where to start. You might already know this, but we called a new preacher a couple of years ago, didn't have no preaching behind him, but a good education at the preacher university. He hardly got on site before he decided he needed bigger training to be called doctor. He enrolled at the University for preachers in Louisville. Did most of his studying on computer down at the church.

"Well, when he had been studying about a year, something come over him. He changed, preached that there would be some pruning at the church. I didn't know what he was talking about, but I knowed what pruning was. First thing you know, people was frowning, leaving directly after the sermon, not talking in the aisles, the parking lot and about. Change was coming alright. I told you what Ethel said about moving ever thing around—pulpit, Lord's Supper table, babies' crying room, where the prayer meeting was held and so forth.

"The preacher even decided that it was his responsibility as to who could join the church, preached that men was to teach, women was to listen. Don't reckon he thought about some of the old boys couldn't read. He even got off on free will, declaring from his reading that ever thing was laid out before the creation. Little children not elected for heaven went to hell. Well, you can probably guess how that all went over. He declared that we shouldn't have business meetings as it caused us to sin. He adjusted the budget without finance committee help."

Before going on, Fred raised a hand and looked inquiringly at his audience, determining if they understood how serious the situation really was. "Then one Sunday night during a heated business meeting something was said negative about the hundred or so that had quit coming, one thing led to another, and first thing you know a great number jumped from their seats, started clapping, and hollering amen to something that was said on the preacher's side. He misjudged the crowd and yelled out that he was a five-point Calvinist, a new version, of course—reformed they call it. Being free-will Congregationalists, that theology didn't set well with the old crowd. He was asked to leave but given some time to get his business in order. That's why he is still around." Fred stood and stretched his legs.

"The women took after him. That's what brought it to a head. Phone calls, emails, letters, women can spread the word, you know. He was smart, good looking, worked hard for a preacher. But he insulted womanhood, you might say. If he'd given the sisters a little wiggle room, we'd never have got rid of him."

I entered W. H.'s room just as he was completing a recitation on something Cicero had said about breaking down institutions by the Emperor, that is, after he had reviewed the Catholic Church's sale of indulgences. The men, looking a bit overwhelmed, rose, shook hands around and left. W. H. and I spent twenty minutes or so, the conversation ranging from his health to the national economy, and, of course, Fred's discourse. W. H. surely repeated it word for word, often stopping to laugh. Again, W. H. did most of the talking. I learned later that he was in court the following morning having left the hospital AMA.

INCARCERATION

Incarceration has haunted man throughout known history. It takes from him his property—including clothing, home, family, and friends, and possibly worst of all, his name. It confines him to a small room, coldly and sparsely furnished among dangerous psychopaths, perverted men, many times harsh, sadistic guards. It withholds the tender touch and sweet voice of female companionship. This is done for institutional safety, for human safety, oftentimes in different parts of the world for the preservation of a despotic system.

Grifton's crime was an attack on the economic institution, specifically the insurance industry. "What I did hurt nobody, except the big insurance company" was a quote he repeated to the locals. Many nodded and agreed. He hadn't really hurt anybody. He had never as much as had a traffic ticket locally, so far as they knew. This mild assessment was contrary to lore that had built up around him over the years. Nevertheless, Grifton was sentenced to federal prison in Manchester, Kentucky.

On my way to Clay County, driving the Hal Rogers Parkway surrounded by hardwoods, coal banks of old still visible in the distance, I was thinking of earlier days. In 1898, reverend Dickie, a traveling Methodist minister-educator, kept a journal of his adventures and observations. His calling he felt was to evangelize and educate the mountain people, and much of his writing, currently reproduced in the *Kentucky Explorer Magazine*, deals with the people of Clay County. He described the bloody disputes, fanned by men of greed and lust for control. Saloons were sites of violent conflicts. Armed gangs supported their cause, usually reflecting family allegiance. Progeny of these leaders and vigilantes are still there, some of whom are currently serving prison terms for vote buying and illegal drug distribution.

However, the people are generally congenial, God-fearing, good looking descendants of Seventeenth Century Virginians left behind in the county during the early Nineteenth Century's great migration west. Their livelihood was derived from timber, salt wells, coal mining, and distilled corn. This insured the continuance of a hearty lot. Clay County's prison currently serves as an economic driver in the absence of local employment opportunities. The timber has been cut over, the salt wells are no longer economically feasible and the coal mining is stalled by new regulations, new mining techniques and alternate energy sources.

At the prison, I was escorted to the office of Andrew Jackson Johnson, Superintendent. Mr. Johnson a man of indeterminate age, grey, muscled, with blue, serious eyes. He greeted me with a too strong grip, I thought. "Mr. Grant, I understand you wish to discuss, Grifton Davis. What may I ask is your interest, your objective? You realize that we are discrete with personal information, I trust."

"Yes, I realize that. I'm writing about Grifton Davis." Then I repeated the conversation I'd had with Grifton about his boys. The Superintendent adjusted his tie, looked down at a stack of papers on his desk, cleared his throat and laughed a hearty laugh. I was a bit taken back, not knowing what he must be thinking.

"You know Grant, you see all types in here from clowns to hard psychopathic killers, rapists, druggies, child abusers, you name it." Johnson was tapping his forefinger on the desk as he talked. "I interviewed Grifton on several occasions. Never saw anyone quite like him. I instinctively knew he was conning me, conning the system, conning the whole world. Yet he was so capable in his personal relationships that the con slipped under the radar. People believed him, believed in him. He cried when he talked about his dear wife's murder, how he had built her dream home, and took in her children. He detailed the workings of his trucking enterprise, his regional sales experience. Did you know he sold cookware at some point? Got to be a self-trained chef. Hell, we put him in charge of the kitchen. That was the only time we've had food fit to eat."

Johnson paused, again looking out the window, apparently thinking about something pertinent. I interrupted. "Mr. Johnson, how did Grifton get on with the staff and fellow inmates? Was he evaluated by the physicians, that is, for personality disorders and so forth?"

"Grant, I can't get into those specifics. I can tell this much. The team read the court background study, the psychiatric social history and searched for a diagnosis, but wound up scratching their heads. Oh, each professional entered his opinion, but these were all over the place. Grifton was a complex man. Court background reports hinted of murder, gambling, bullying, drug sales. The list is long. But I can unequivocally say this, Grifton Davis was a model prisoner."

Johnson laid his hands on the desk in front of him, palms up as he said this. "Grifton worked hard, supported staff decisions, abided by prison rules. To my knowledge he never had an angry encounter with another inmate—which is saying something, I'm here to tell you." Again, the superintendent laughed, his body shaking. "He was probably one of very few men who left prison to cheers from both inmates and staff, with considerably more money than he came with. It was reported he raised small sums every day, gambling with the guards as well as the inmates. People said he'd bet on anything—where a fly would light next, how long before a cloud would obscure the sun, you name it.

One other thing though, he admitted his crime, that it was illegal and wrong, but rationalized that it really wasn't all that bad. No blood was spilled. No widow woman deprived. No children mistreated. No personal property stolen. Insurance companies, according to Grifton, accumulated their money just as he did, by gambling. He went on to say that financiers, many of them from the insurance world, bundled mortgages drawn against poor people, sold them worldwide, and locked up finance around the globe, nearly starving us all out. 'Now that was a crime,' he said. Oh, he also asked, 'and what happened to that financier bunch'?" At that, Mr. Johnson looked at his watch and declared the meeting over.

I left the prison with some information but little that I didn't already know. I had wanted to speak with a cellmate or a prison guard, a cook in the kitchen. Rumor was that computers, the big boxy style, opened for repairs after he was discharged, contained contraband including handmade weapons, drugs, money, and numbers records all stored in the casings. I was curious as to any role Grifton might have played in this, for example. Also, what had he done with his scammed money? Did he admit to any other crimes? Who came up with the insurance scheme? Who visited him?

GAMBLING FRIENDS

I traveled from Berea in Madison County, Kentucky east by northeast for several miles through the Knobs, geologically labeled as erosional remnants of mountains. Knobs here describe moderate-sized hills, wooded bottom to top. I'm driving through a sweeping valley, lush with summer grass, fat cattle grazing in neatly fenced fields. Farm houses sit back from the road. An occasional ranch style house is built much closer to the road, and by the fencing looks to have a five or so acre plot. These houses are occupied by offspring of the farmers, or by gardeners and horse lovers who have renounced the town life. The view on either side of the wide valley features the hills, each separated by narrow hollows, and each knob rising at a steep grade for maybe five hundred plus feet, then flat on top—more like mounds than hills.

Still in search of Grifton: seeking his old haunts, hoping for interviews, experiences that might get him to speak that I might know the real man. Discussions thus far reveal a composite of the man established by locals, mere coffee shop rumors, I think, and of questionable veracity.

The road narrowed, barely allowing two cars to pass, then my GPS called for a left turn onto a still narrower gravel lane heading directly toward two hills. I was stopped by a closed farm gate. The gate blocked access to what appeared to be a passable dirt road—two gravel paths matched the vehicle tires. I had been advised to close the gate after entering. The road wound around one of the Knobs and inclined slightly as it passed between the hills. This was one of the hollows, and like most hollows it sloped higher in elevation than the valley. Red clover and orchard grass grew on both sides over to the woods.

Just out of sight of the main valley was the house, my destination. It was constructed of logs, sawed and stained, a long, deep porch extending across the front deep enough to shelter visitors from summer rains and seat fifty or so people. A carved wooden door, featuring a variety of wildlife, and much higher and wider than the standard, provided entrance to the house. Crit Rose, the man I had talked to at a restaurant in Richmond answered the door, smiling. He was maybe five-six, fit, fine brown hair hanging down over his forehead, grey eyes. "Come in Caleb. How was the drive? Have any trouble finding me? How about something to drink?"

The rapid-fire questions stopped me for a second. "Fine, no, yes, thank you, maybe a glass of water." I hoped the answers were in the right sequence and made sense. I followed him to a long counter which separated the cooking area from the living area. This part of the house was completely open. It had the same finish as the outside and featured the longest overhead beam extending the length of the great room that I had ever seen. Grove Park Inn near Ashville, North Carolina came to mind.

"So, you're interested in Grifton Davis. I knew him over a few years, saw him three or four times a year. We gathered here now and then." Crit handed me the water and gestured for me to sit on a deep, soft leather couch. Some distance off to my right was a highly polished table, cherry I think, with five comfortable-looking chairs.

Crit continued, "I see you are looking at our game table. Five men play at each game. At those Grifton games, the chair closest to you belonged to Bell County, a tall slender fellow, never took his John Deere cap off, wore leather work boots." Crit looked down and smiled at this revelation. "To his right sat Paducah, dressy casual mostly, bright cardigans, wool slacks. Next was Detroit, black silk shirt, red silk tie, diamond stick pin, slicked hair." Crit gave me a knowing look, like you know what that means. "The slightly taller chair was Grifton's, a specialty item built to accommodate long legs. He always came in smiling, his wavy black hair shining, those black eyes taking everything in. Usually had a set of dice jiggling them in his right hand. Wore the same shirt design every time—brown with a large flower pattern, something from the Pacific probably. And, of course, the last chair was mine. I was home so I dressed Florida comfortable." I had no idea why it was important to him that I know how each man dressed—possibly just conversation.

Crit looked out the window across the room toward the mound mountain. "Beautiful, isn't it? The hills, I mean. Knew I had to be here the first visit to the area. Came up from Florida and met the county attorney over in Estill County. He invited me out to the house for a barbeque. He sold me the house and acreage before I left the area. Just came up for a few days to turkey hunt. Funny how fate works isn't it. I still have property in Florida, go down during January and February." I must have looked at him inquiringly. He added, "I have a farm manager and house keeper who look after this." He gestured across the great room and toward the wide windows revealing land that sloped gently toward the knob.

I nodded, set my glass on the table and asked Crit to tell me how their game worked. He looked at me and smiled.

"There's not much to tell. It began on Friday evening and ended sometime Monday morning. It was a spree actually—beautiful attendants, good food, lots of spirits. We broke for a smoke and drink every few hours, sometimes taking time to dance with the attendants." He held both hands up and made quotation signs when he said attendants.

"Oh, and, there was a twenty-thousand-dollar cover charge, deposited with the door guard on entrance. This deposit, so to speak, was granted to the winner. That's money over and above his winnings, less, of course, food, attendant pay and other incidentals. Attendants aren't cheap, you know." Crit looked at me and winked as he said the last. This was big stuff in my world.

Crit seemed to think for a second. "Grifton was the character of the group, the man to beat, too. If he dealt, he won the pot when he desired. We all watched his every move, trying to see just how it worked. Decks were changed. Cards were cut. No matter, he was still in control. He had the fastest hands I ever saw. Cards snapped around the table. His fingers never seemed to move. When someone else dealt, he more times than not knew who had the winning hand, how strong it was and continued to take the pot seemingly at will. Oh, now and again, he'd let one of us come out with the night's chips, just to keep us playing. It sometimes took months to overcome our loses." He laughed and moved to pour a drink. He asked if I wanted one. I declined. Then as he poured, he said over his shoulder, "We all knew he cheated, but no one ever figured out how. Bell County once said, 'Grifton could make a deck of cards dance a waltz, if he was so-minded'." Crit's Assessment of Grifton's play was likely inflated, but obviously fun for Crit to tell as he played out much of the action parts with hand and body movements.

Wanting to expand the discussion, I asked if he would still play with Grifton in the group. "Hell, yes, he was the most interesting man I ever met. Seemed to be able to read people's minds." Crit didn't dismiss me after these last remarks, but I sensed the interview was over. We talked about his house and land as he let me out, following me onto the porch. He was standing looking across the meadow at the knobs as I drove away. A lonely man, I thought.

Before reaching the entrance gate I met three cars, none of which gave an inch of the drive. I moved to a gently sloping ditch as the big Mercedes, the Suburban, and the Lincoln Navigator passed, their windows darkened. At the farm gate entry, I was greeted by a fleshy, bearded man who opened and waved me through. He hadn't been there when I arrived, neither had the travel trailer parked near the fence—apparently a portable guardhouse. I began to have second thoughts about Crit being lonely.

Something else was nagging though. Sometime back I'd had a business dealing with a young man named Delbert Yarbrough. Delbert had served in the marines in one of the Middle East campaigns, attended college a year or so, and dropped out to gamble fulltime. I thought of him as Mountain rather than Delbert. His arms were bigger than my thigh, his round head suited only for a toboggan, too large for any hat I'd ever observed. He was equally strong, shifting, rolling large logs as we sawed.

I ask Delbert about his gambling. "I was good," he said.

"Did you ever know Grifton Davis?" I raised this doubting that they had met due to the age difference.

"I sure did." Delbert went on to tell me about gambling with Grifton.

"You actually went up against Grifton? How did you fare?" I asked the latter, while thinking, probably not so well.

"Grifton was pretty good. I could beat him if we had a stationary dealer. Won twenty-one hundred dollars off him the last time we played." Delbert had to have been in his twenties to have played against Delbert. I was impressed. I asked him why he specified a stationary dealer.

"Grifton cheated. If he dealt, his hands were so quick and accurate he always managed cards in the deck. The ones he wanted, he got. I remember one time playing *tonk* with him. I got two Jacks. Played out the hand and the other Jacks never showed. Cards were left on the table. I picked them up for examination. The other two Jacks weren't there. Not wanting a scene, I just said, I'm out. Grifton was getting old by that time, you know." Delbert dropped his head as he said this.

"Any idea where the Jacks were?" I was intrigued but still a little suspicious.

Delbert looked past me as though studying the timber we were cruising. "Grifton was so slick, he placed cards under his leg, up his sleeve, you name it. I never knew of anyone catching him at this though." Delbert's eyes were twinkling now, a big smile on his face. "I caught him without seeing how he did it and he knew I'd caught him. We never had any trouble after that." This wasn't altogether new information. But it, along with the Crit discussion, confirmed the gambling circuit.

Delbert provided a firsthand experience. He appeared to be trustworthy, yet accepting that a twenty-something year old played such a role against Grifton—embellished? I wondered.

On the drive home, I was in a quandary. Grifton was still a mystery, the dichotomy—evil yet caring. Each interview supported the *historical narrative* picked up in the community. Only Forrest had provided new information. My inclination now was to attempt a conversation with Forrest's siblings. One is rumored to be in prison. He is an unlikely source. I don't know what I might face with any of the rest.

SCAM

My hopes were sagging. No member of Grifton's family was currently available, thus hopes of getting him to speak through them appeared bleak. Then on a Saturday evening I was walking along the lake road past Forrest's house. I noted several people on the porch—Forrest, his wife, an elderly lady, two young children. I waved and walked on not wishing to interrupt the visit. I hadn't traveled but a few feet when Forrest came off the porch and hailed me. His wife, a slight lady of medium height, bare feet, and wearing a blond ill-fitting wig, followed several steps behind.

Forrest pointed out the new paint on the porch foundation. He'd had it done earlier in the day. "Looks better, don't it?" Forrest punched his chin toward me. as he said this. His wife moved directly in front of me, her hand extended for me to shake.

"What do you think about him ruining my porch?" she asked.

Forrest took a step back, "She don't like it that I had it painted." With that, the wife again shook my hand and moved back to the porch. I thought her eyes and movement might betray over-medication.

"That's my aunt and her grandchildren." He gestured toward the porch.

Just then a car wheeled into the drive traveling at a pretty good pace to make the turn, causing Forrest and me to step farther into the grass; a beautiful Corvette, not new, but extremely well-cared for. Forrest's sister, a thin lady, about Forrest's height, with long black curls, dark eyes stepped from the vehicle into the yard and was introduced.

"He bought Dad's houseboat." Forrest pointed this out to the sister after introductions and a brief discussion regarding the relationship between Forrest and me—good friends, according to Forrest. I nodded agreement.

"You got a good boat." She smiled rather bleakly, I
thought. "Good to meet you, Mr. Grant," she said and
walked to the porch. I continued with Forrest.
"He did build an excellent boat," I said, mainly to keep the
discussion moving. Forrest was looking at me as though the
conversation wasn't finished.
"Had a lot of metal in it, built by a man from Madison
county, but Dad supervised ever weld." I complimented
Forrest on his house and how neat he kept the huge expanse
of yard sloping back to the lake.
"I had a new house down on Highway 290, paid for before
I was twenty-five years old. The government took it, you
know." I didn't know. This was new information.
"Government took Sis's house, too." No emotion was
apparent as Forrest gave this information.
"How did that happen?" I asked somewhat hesitantly.
"You know about Dad's trouble with the law and the
insurance company, don't you?" I nodded. "They said I
was his son. She was his daughter, so they took both
houses." I had heard about the children's property being
purchased and developed by Grifton but didn't know which
children. In fact, I had heard that three children were sent to
prison along with Grifton. Forrest continued, "I went to
Federal prison for two years. Everbody works in Federal,
you know. If you are blind, don't matter. They put you to
filling salt-shakers or something.
"There was one fellow there, his kin had been a big shot,
anyway, controlled government appointments. Big man.
They put him in the hole six times while I was there
because he wouldn't work. He said, 'I didn't pick up papers
on the outside and am not going to in here.'" Forrest
chuckled.
"He was a big hefty fellow when he came in, about like
me." Forrest rubbed his stomach which stretched his tee
shirt considerably. "He lost a hundred pounds, grew his
beard down to here." Forrest slashed his hand across his

midsection, just above his beltless trousers. "Something else, the big shot's kin wouldn't accept placement in a halfway house; said he wanted to do his time, and then he wanted them to 'leave him to hell alone.'" Forrest looked down, spit on the ground and smiled.

"The doctor involved with Dad's work went to the pen too. They said he had doctors working for him while he was in lock-up. A church group came down to visit him every Sunday. Oh, and one other thing, it was reported that that doctor bilked Medicaid out of millions of dollars—that put some money in circulation, didn't it?" Forrest looked intently at me as he asked this question.

"Forrest, if it doesn't bother you to talk about it, I'd like to stop by sometime and hear more details as to how the scam worked," I extended my hand for a shake and to end our discussion. "I don't want to interfere further with your family visit."

"I'll tell you anything I know. It don't bother me. God bless you." Forrest held on to my hand. "You know he didn't hurt nobody. Put a lot of money in the county. He had a whole bunch of people working for him." I had heard figures twenty-five to fifty but was sure if Forrest didn't know the exact count probably nobody else did either.

The discussion left me wondering about Forest always ending our discussions with, "God bless you." Scam artist to religious witness. A man can change, I decided. I walked on home excited, delighted that at last I might be getting somewhere with the investigation. However, a systematic inquiry without a paper trail, dependent on loosely connected information, or likely biased family members reports makes for a questionable outcome.

That was Saturday evening when Forrest and I had the discussion. On Sunday, after worship services I was talking with James Madison Clark, a retired police chief with whom I had worked when I was in politics. "I have got some red oak and walnut lumber that you might be interested in looking at," I said. James had taken up woodwork after retirement and had become quite proficient in building furniture.

"I had one of the Yarbrough boys bring his portable mill in and saw a few logs. Yarbrough and I are already working on another project," I added. The lumber came from a red oak that fell during a wind storm, and a walnut that grew along the bank of a wet weather stream. Over the years the wet seasons run-off eroded the bank and the walnut fell across the fence into the horse pasture. The logs didn't saw out much, maybe five hundred board feet, but both trees were solid and I couldn't just let them go to waste.

"Yeah, I'd be interested in some of the red oak. You know what they want for a finished eight-foot board at Lowes? Several dollars, I'll tell you." James' voice got even deeper. We agreed for him come to my house the following morning for coffee. "Black," he said. "We'll appraise the lumber."

James arrived promptly at nine as we had agreed. "Good, hot, black coffee, just the way I like it." James was in a good mood. He is a huge man, closer to three hundred pounds than two, at least six feet three, excellent man for handling rowdies as an officer of the law. He is also one of the kindest, most sensitive men I've ever known. No reports of police brutality on his watch.

We drank our coffee and proceeded to the barn to view the lumber. "How much you want for the red oak?" James picked up one end of a board and rubbed it with his hand. They were one by twelve by thirteen feet long.

"I'll tell you what James, I'll give you a few boards, enough to build a piece. Then if you want more, we'll talk about it. How's that?" James is a very accommodating man, always ready to assist widows in emergencies, or anybody else, for that matter. I couldn't bring myself to charge him.

"Can't beat that," he replied.

We retired to the barn porch with comfortable chairs, a swing and various grandchildren's riding toys, parked in a row. The horse nickered at the fence nearby and brought on considerable discussion.

"We were poor, never could have a horse." James looked sad when he said this, then continued. "We did have a dog when us children came home from the orphanage." James had told me a few years earlier about him and his sisters being placed in a Louisville orphanage for some years. "Dad had the dog, a hound. We couldn't get close to it. Durn thing would eat you up. It finally got killed on the highway, but not before having a litter. We got to keep one. That dog got grown and protected us children just like a good baby sitter."

The talk continued and finally came around to where I lived, then to my buying Grifton's boat which was now moored in our sight down on the waterway. James gave me an inquiring look. "You knew about us breaking the case against Grifton on the insurance fraud, didn't you?" He was staring at me, looking very serious.

"No, I sure didn't!" I answered, my excitement showing.

"Sure enough did. One of the officers in my department investigated a wreck on Main Street, just a fender bender, involving Forrest Davis, Grifton's son, and I can't remember who the other party was." I was now leaning in, on the edge of my chair to be certain of hearing how this tied with the scam. "The officer was discussing the accident with the parties when Grifton appeared. 'Don't call the insurance people or write a report,' he requested. 'I'll pay to get your car repaired.' Grifton made this last remark to the fellow Forrest had hit. The officer looked at the man who nodded and said, okay. A little against protocol, but the officer agreed. I later discussed it with the officer, questioning why Grifton insisted on no insurance representative or police report. It became clearer to us sometime later."

I asked James what happened.

"Well, a second accident was investigated out on Highway 80 sometime later, and again, Forrest was in the car. The report showed this, and the insurance people noted that Forrest was supposed to be in the hospital here in Kentucky, I think. I'm not sure just where." James looked at me and shook his head. "Something wasn't right," he said. "Forrest had a policy that paid the owner so much a day when hospitalized. Payments were being made to Forrest. The Doctor filed the claim, but Forrest was not hospitalized. One thing led to another and the fraud was uncovered. Grifton had a Doctor with privileges in some hospital. The doctor maintained medical records on Grifton's so-called employees, who in turn got the five hundred dollars a day or whatever the policy called for and shared the spoils with both Grifton and the Doctor. That took a lot of claims to amount to sums reported—in the millions."

I whistled out a breath and moved to get up from my chair. "Now, wait just a minute." James raised his hand to stay me, and said, "I don't how much of this to believe." He then began a more bizarre story.

Grifton's cousin, Albert, also profited from the insurance scam. He could have been involved at the time Grifton was indicted, or earlier. James didn't know for sure. The report indicated that Albert bought nearly fifty of the daily-pay policies, then faked an accident—rear-ended auto possibly. James didn't know since the story hadn't provided that specific. Albert was admitted to the hospital for ninety days. A regular health insurance policy paid the hospital while the daily policies paid him over seven thousand dollars per day. Albert's ruse was discovered and he was fined one hundred and fifty thousand dollars. He paid with a cashier's check.

James finished this story and looked intently at me as though to say, "Some investment wasn't it?"

"Did he do any prison time," I inquired? James shook his head no. Did he use the same hospital and doctor as Grifton's other associates? Again, James shook his head and said he didn't know. How could any one person buy fifty policies? I was bumfuzzled.

"The reason I said in the beginning that I couldn't vouch for the truthfulness of this story is that I can't answer your questions." James was picking at what appeared to be a splinter in his palm: "The whole durn scheme is unbelievable, but we know some variation of it happened. Aha," James blurted out, and examined a small dark sliver on his knife blade.

My wife called from the back porch beckoning me to the house to pay a neighbor boy for the morning's yard-work. James and I strolled through the yard, and around the house to his truck. Standing on the front drive, we agreed to get together soon for more coffee and talk—as we patted each other on the shoulder.

GRIFTON'S NEIGHBOR

The recent meetings with Forrest and J. M. Clark, the former police, chief gave me new hope in the search for the real Grifton. Red Franklin, a long-time neighbor, was the next one I thought about and subsequently called. I told Red that I was Caleb Grant and asked if he remembered me.

"You bet I do. How are you doing?" Pleasantries were exchanged, and I got to the issue of Grifton. Red acknowledged remembering me, but I thought by his voice that he might not. We had met a few times at the cattle market where he visited weekly to spread his trade goods in the parking lot with what seemed to be hundreds of other traders. Everything from live chickens, hoe handles, rugs, saddles, knives, and what looked to be AK47s were sold and traded. Red traded some place nearly every day on most anything.

"Red I'd like to come down and visit with you for a bit. I'm gathering information on Grifton Davis."

"I thought his case was over and buried with him." Red said this in his usual slow drawl. His drawl certainly didn't mean slow thought, however. He had retired some years ago from the airlines industry, apparently a very successful career according to his life style. The buying, selling, trading was strictly a hobby, a successful one. Interestingly, no one I knew ever accused him of cheating. He merely knew how, and what to buy at a reasonable price, and then sell reasonably.

"I'm not looking-into Grifton from a legal standpoint. Grifton made a request sometime before his passing that I give his then young sons a report on him. Since you were his neighbor for years, I wanted to talk with you about him—just for those boys."

"Oh, I see. Sure, I'd be glad to assist anyway I can. Haven't heard much good about the boys though." Red didn't go further, but I knew he was referring to the school burning, and maybe drug issues.

"When would be a good time for me to come by?" I was hoping today.

"Well, Caleb, I can't meet this morning. I'm scheduled to meet a fellow in Knoxville to look about a warehouse of goods I bought." Red laughed, a little embarrassed maybe. "Bought it over the internet, subject to inspection. I might meet you early this evening, say 6:30." We agreed on the time and I hung up the phone and headed to the horse pasture to mend fence.

The complex adjacent to the horse pasture has a large lawn. Their yard men often hang mower decks on the fence face-boards, jerk them off, and ride on. Also, the horse loves to travel to that side of the field where people give him treats. If someone walks close to the fence and doesn't give him attention or a treat, he has a habit of pushing until a board or two pops off or breaks. This morning as I bent over tacking a board back onto the post, JD, the horse, snatched my hat and ran—part of the cost of keeping a pet horse.

Early that evening, I drove down on Highway 70 to Red's house. "Red, it's good to see you." I had stopped at the house but Red's wife directed me to a shed set back some distance, but still on the property.

"Come on in, Caleb. I'd offer you a chair, but the best I've got is that other five-gallon bucket over there." We both laughed, and I sat across from him, that is, across on the far side of a tarp on the
ground. On it was a pile of new pliers, screw drivers, hammers, hacksaws, you name it. Red waved his hand over his treasure, "This is a sample of what I bought in Knoxville today. Reckon I'll ever sell a warehouse full of such?" Red had a glint in eye. He knew he'd sell it.

The shed was a long affair, one story, built in the board and batten style with huge garage doors on each end. Three isles ran the length of the building, and I could see lawn equipment, garden tools, outside furniture, horse tack, tires, transmission fluid, paint, and that was in just one isle. Red was picking up various pieces, examining the metal, running his finger along sharp edges, clicking switches, but most intently, he looked at the trade marks, looking for forged metal objects made in small USA foundries. These he laid aside, knowing their worth to represent a five or six hundred per cent mark-up. "Look at this set of open-end wrenches mixed in the China-made pile—all the same price." He gave me a knowing grin.

"You didn't come here to look at a pile of tools though, did you?"

"No, however, your retirement hobby/work is interesting, and I see that you enjoy it. As we discussed on the phone, I, am doing retirement work too, but much less profitable, I assure you." I picked up a knife sharpener and examined it, considering whether it was appropriate for pocket knives. "Where did Grifton Davis live when he was your neighbor?"

"Right across the road there." He pointed down the gravel drive toward a house across the road. Grifton had lived next to Red for several years before building a house in town. "Everybody knew he was a character. When he was building that house, he used to come over and sit with me sometimes. He always filled me in on every detail the workmen had completed that day. Some said he paid the contractor every Friday in crisp one-hundred-dollar bills. I know where he got some of his money. I'll tell you something though, you couldn't ask for a better neighbor." Red had a very serious look as he said this.

I asked Red about his statement as to "where Grifton got some of his money." This could be new stuff. I was engaged. I wanted to hear.

"I bought a Fredric Remington Bronze from Grifton several years ago. Only it wasn't bronze, it was pure silver—The Bronco Buster, a very low numbered cast. I had no idea how much it was worth, but I found one listed on line for fifty thousand. He wanted twelve, so I took a chance, insured it for twenty-five, and stored it in the back of my gun case. According to gossip, he may not have paid anything for it, won it in a game."

"That was profitable," I said, "that is, if he sure enough didn't have any money in it". I knew a little more than I revealed at the time.

"Actually—Grifton and I both made money, I suppose." Red chuckled as he said this. A large Collie dog strolled into the shed, his silky coat shinning, his tail wagging slowly. He smelled my hand in passing, then went over and laid his head in Red's lap.

"Funny thing happened. Someone broke into my house and stole that statute. Shook the wife and me up—not that we missed the object, or lost any money, it's just the thought of someone coming into the house. Nothing else was touched. We bought an expensive security system after that." Red wiped his forehead with his handkerchief as he made this comment.

I noticed the security sign in the yard, and, also, I saw the shed cameras. I had heard about the theft. Nobody ever connected Grifton with it though, even in coffee shop gossip. It did happen directly after Grifton was released from prison. His possible involvement ran through my mind. I had told Red on the phone about gathering information to be passed on to those boys. I now expressed my desire to get some positive comments from acquaintances.

"I understand perfectly." Red tossed a screw driver back onto the pile as he said this. "You know, Caleb, I'll tell you what I know. About the only thing I can say is that Grifton Davis was a wonderful neighbor, a perfect gentleman around the wife and me. He helped in every charity we were involved in, gave liberally to people around who fell on hard times. He was gone an awful lot—out buying, gambling, whatever it was he did. I wish I knew more."

Red wiped his hand on his coverall leg, removing new-tool grease. The remainder of our talk involved Red's interest in my background and my interest in his. His range of travels with the airlines left me feeling quite parochial.

As I traveled toward home, my mind raced through each interview: Hard working dad; interesting man who likely cheated at cards; more than a survivor during incarceration; well liked; considerate of others; created a lot of jobs, put money in circulation. All of this has been reported by first-hand observers, observers who spent time close to Grifton. Juxtaposed to these reports though, I have the rumors, unanimous in reporting personality rot and mayhem, a fraudulent conniver.

On arriving home, I found a note my wife, Mandy, had left asking that I call Red. Anticipating something new I immediately placed the call.

"Caleb, after you left here, the wife and I got to talking about Grifton. She told me something I thought you might get a kick out of. She said Mrs. Jacobs, our next-door neighbor once told her of a discussion she had with him." At this Red stopped and laughed heartedly, briefly losing his breath. "She said, Grifton told her that, 'people say a lot of things about me, but actually, I'm a good man'. Thought you'd want to know that."

We both laughed and ended the conversation. Is it possible that a man can be outside societal norms in his treatment of others, in his business practices and still honestly consider himself good? I'll have to study some on this.

THE OBSESSION

Ordinarily after giving thanks for a good night's sleep, and considering what day it is, I usually try to think what is pressing to be done. Not this morning, my thoughts were confined to Grifton, Ace, and Duce. Grifton hadn't made a death-bed request that I report to his boys as to his accomplishments, character or whatever. It was several years after his request that his son Forrest approached me at a friend's wedding. "If you want to see Dad, you'd better go soon."

Forrest had grown up out of my sight, so I really didn't know who he was or who he was talking about. I   did manage the conversation without embarrassing either of us and inquired of a mutual friend standing nearby who he was. Forrest was identified for me. The friend also explained that his dad, Grifton, was dying of cancer. I didn't go see Grifton, but suddenly now years later, I'm burdened for Ace and Duce. I wish I had made the visit. Grifton might have released me from my commitment had I made that visit.

At this late date I decided to temper any report to the Davis men, realizing that they likely knew enough bad stuff, and fearing that the bad stuff had become glamorized, enticing mimicking on their part. One thing I felt very strongly about though was their likelihood of rationalizing illegal behavior—even actions that are wrong but maybe not illegal. The report must somehow address this. I could not get my mind to go someplace else. The Grifton family issue was controlling me this morning.

Obsessing, I needed help, maybe even counseling. Throughout breakfast, then when trying to read the news, and later when retrieving mail from the box, my mind was running through alternate scenarios. So about ten o'clock, I decided to try and meet with W. H. An unlikely psychological counselor, or sage for that matter; however, he has a settling effect on me. So, I rather sheepishly called him.

"Hello, W. H., this is Caleb Grant." As I made the call I was picturing Grifton at the Chevron Station, in his hat, surrounded by friends and making his plea that had begun to control my mind. My hand trembled slightly, not because of the mind picture, but because I had to give W. H. a sensible reason for calling him.

"Why, hello, Caleb, to what do I owe this early call from such a busy man of the city gates?" The greeting, over the top as W. H's greetings usually were, relieved my anxiety somewhat. As to my being a leader at the city gates, no. I merely write a human-interest piece now and then for the local weekly paper and attend meetings of local planning or care-giving boards.

"W. H., I've got something bothering me, and a man of your legal knowledge might help." As this now seemingly stupid statement came out, I was looking through the window beyond my desk. I noticed Amos Moon driving by, his head leaned forward over the steering wheel, which he turned slightly one way, then the other almost rhythmically as he passed.

"Caleb, you haven't skinned one of the town fathers or been thrown out by the wife, I hope." W. H. said this while removing a brief from the office copier that had to be filed with the court before noon.

"Oh, no. Could I come and talk with you?" I hardly knew what else to say since my problem suddenly seemed so adolescent, especially to present to a busy attorney.

"Hellfire, come on over to the coffee shop next to my office. I'll be there within five minutes or so. Always time for a learned friend." Busy or not W. H. was usually ready to sit and expound.

W. H. was sitting with his elbows on the table, reading what I assumed was a legal brief when I got to the coffee shop. After some preliminaries, I phrased my question. I didn't mention my mental state though but suspected he could detect my distress. "W. H., what is the essence of law?"

W. H. sat back in his chair, looked intently at me and said, "Hellfire, Caleb what kind of question is that? You want a curbside opinion, I suppose." I'm sure W. H. detected my wilted look. I explained that my report to Ace and Duce about Grifton should address the issue of rationalizing illegal behavior.

"Wait, wait! I think I can quote something that possibly will shed some light on your question." W. H. changed his demeanor completely, removed his glasses, looked down at the table, pinched his nose.

As he thought, so did I. After some snooping and several interviews, the burden of summarizing something that I could report to Ace and Duce was still out of reach, so in desperation, I had called W. H. For a minute, I wished I hadn't, but since Grifton could so easily rationalize his behavior, I suspected the boys had adopted this same line of thinking, and maybe W. H. could help me sort through it.

"I think I've got it! Hold just a second. Ah, yes. The great Cicero said it very succinctly: 'The law is right reason in agreement with nature. It is of universal application, unchanging and everlasting. It summons to duty by its commands and averts from wrongdoing by its prohibitions'."

Oh, great, was my first thought. How in the world could this definition be used to shed light on my question? "W. H., that's impressive—being able to pull that up from memory. It leaves me in a quandary, however."

"I think I might know what got you off track." W. H. removed his glasses, licked each lens and buffed them with his handkerchief. "You are wondering how the law is absolute yet gets reinterpreted in nearly every courtroom. Right?"

"Something like that, yes."

"I've asked myself that question many times. For example, a man is in court for making one hundred proof moonshine whiskey in a dry county. Just a mile away in a neighboring county, a fellow makes his living selling one hundred proof whiskey with no interference. Now, is it right to send one to an Atlanta prison and let the other go free about his business?"

My answer is, "Yes, the tax issue comes into play."

W. H. says, "Is it a good law that under any circumstance it is wrong to sell alcohol?" I respond, no, but it is wrong not to pay taxes on the product.

"Now," W. H. continues, "my defendant can't pay taxes on his product, it's against the law in his so-called dry county. You see, Caleb, things aren't so absolute, are they?"

"W. H. you may be explaining a lot, but none of it seems to help my case," I said. A chubby waitress approached our table. W. H. was preoccupied thinking, so he didn't acknowledge her. She smiled and winked at me not flirting, but in a watch this sort of way. She bent over W. H., refilled his cup as she massaged his shoulder. She then planted a kiss on top of his near bald head, and grinned at me as if to say, he never notices. In fact, W. H. didn't change his composure, or acknowledge her being there.

"Caleb, let me put it another way. A man owes a sum of money. He has mortgaged his only mule on which the livelihood of his family is totally dependent. The argument is to make him sell his mule, and pay the obligation; however, it is known that the sale will not completely settle his indebtedness. He has made payments monthly. An emergency put him in a hard spot. He is now behind three months. Do you make him sell the mule and starve? Or do you let him keep the mule and pay once his emergency ends? The first choice leaves the creditors short on full payment, and the defendant's family destitute, the second choice while not absolute, gives possible satisfaction to both defendant and plaintiff."

"W. H. you are very willing to assist, to get people to think on complex issues, but I'm afraid I just can't follow the arguments to a definitive answer to my question. If Ace and Duce go through life rationalizing the law to their benefit, then I haven't done them any favor with the report."

"Hellfire, Caleb, you can't take responsibility for raising those boys. Besides, they are men now. Just tell them that Grifton built some good houses, and lost them when he went to jail, that he sold melons, coal, jewels, that he got some bad things said about him. In summary, he broke the law and went to jail—just two simple sentences. Don't let it drive you nuts. Most of us are near that precipice over something from time to time, you know." I wondered about the implications of the last statement.

"I know this may be frustrating for a man like you, W. H., but when I hear absolute or natural law, I think of murder. Surely forbidding that is natural law, or maybe it's Biblical law. Don't do this, don't do that. And, finally I think of pre-Civil War law and slavery, about the Declaration of Independence stating that 'all men are created equal'."

"Hold right there. Remember each case is adjudicated one at a time. No two cases are the same. Slavery was legal according to the law." W. H. placed his elbows on the table, his hands up and clasp before his face.

"A perfect example of what disturbs me," I said. "How was legalized slavery an absolute or natural law, unless slaves were not human; can a person with human blood not be human? Was it natural before emancipation and not everlasting after? Was Cicero right that law is everlasting and unchanging? How could people be considered just a fraction of a man for census taking?" The coffee shop hub-bub seemed to leave us unnoticed. We were isolated, occupied.

"Caleb, I possibly got us on the wrong tract with Cicero. Let's consider Biblical law. The greatest judge ever challenged the brilliant legal minds regarding the Sabbath. The Pharisees quoted the no work on the Sabbath issue. They condemned Christ, the ultimate judge, for eating; and, for curing the infirmed. Christ, in turn, pointed out that King David had eaten the temple shew bread. Surely his follower's gathering a few grains from a farmer's field (which was legal) for nourishment on the Sabbath was okay; a lamb in a pit must be rescued even on the Sabbath. The conclusion: to do good, to show mercy is legal even on the Sabbath. Shows love for man, consideration for life in God's creation." We sat quietly for some time, each studying our coffee cups.

"Pardon me, but I'm going to have to run over to the courthouse and file this motion right quick." W. H. waved his sheaf of papers and tugged his way up, scraping his chair on the hardwood floor. "Let's continue this conversation soon. Maybe I'll have something more appropriate to say."

We shook hands. I thanked him and we each went our way, thinking about the law—him his next case, me just wondering. What had Grifton really meant by "tell my boys about me"? Was it house of Grifton? The psychologic Grifton? W. H's. two sentence Grifton?

Even though I hadn't got what I'd hoped to for my expanding report, the discussion, W. H.'s presence had calmed my mind considerably. Just talking with a calming personality even if the talk had been far afield from present concerns had yielded dividends.

LOCATING THE BOYS

In my world I see people leave their houses early to motor off to their work: to area factories, to health care facilities, to government offices, to schools, or to small businesses. On Sundays, they go to church or to recreation spots. Retirees knot around tables at the McDonalds. Housewives beat rugs on the front drive. Fathers pass ball with their children. Most people I know are productive, have a purpose in life, have an interest in books, political news, world events, child rearing, proper diet, sports. But as I age, I now realize that my head travels above a cloud that hides a great deal just below. A second cloud above me hides just as much. Those above the cloud over my head jet around the world at will, race multimillion dollar horses, sleep in two-thousand dollar a night rooms, or wear fifty thousand-dollar outfits.

In my search for Ace and Duce it's the dark cloud below me that must be penetrated. Get down among the felons, the drop outs. At my request, W. H. inquired around the court house about the two boys. Their burning the school some years ago I feared was just the beginning. Likely neither of them had experienced the joys of back yard barbeques, beach volley ball, a day at the ball park, church services on Sunday, bird watching, hiking the Appalachian trail, caring for a wife and family.

In my mind they were more likely to be in a trailer on the outskirts, approached by a path leading through the droppings of previous and current occupants, droppings that they were going to get back to—a lawnmower deck, a used automobile tire, parts from a child's swing set, soft drink cans, beer bottles, syringes, all left not stacked, just dropped for the weeds and grass to grow up around and over; the trailer door rusted through across the bottom, sagging, hard to open. Window openings have no glass, plastic once taped to resist elements now tattered, blowing in the breeze. Inside the trailer I picture pizza boxes with mold-covered crusts scattered about on coffee tables, or counter tops, empty plastic that once held munchies, plastic baggies once containing pot, meth, or opioids now empty and kicked about. The electricity is off. Water does not flow from the facets. Young people are sprawled on dirty bedding, couches, recliners, and on the floor. The scene is much like a movie-set depicting an outlaw camp led by a dirty-footed, weak leader. It's here that one is most likely to find Ace and Duce, I feared—not today, however.

The boy's current habitat is the county jail. W. H. reported in our recent discussion that Ace was in jail here in the county, Duce in Clark County. I'll have to get my head down under the cloud at my feet if I'm to meet the two as they weave their way among countless others who survive just as wretchedly.

I go back to Forrest. "They conned Dad out of a lot of money at the end." That was his first response to my query. "I was there when they came with their hand out. Caleb, you can't finance such people. They'll break-up anybody and everybody within their circuit." Forrest's presence during these visits lends considerable credence to his report. Yet, his reports, do seem a bit over the top in presentation as do most presentations by practiced story tellers.

Forrest began his story quoting Ace. "'Hey, Pops, anything to eat in the house?' He'd burst into Dad's house. He didn't even acknowledge me." Forest lowered his head. "He passed Dad's recliner without further comment—heading to the kitchen. Ace hadn't been to see Dad in several months even though the old man was dying of cancer and bound to his bed or recliner. On a previous visit Ace had convinced Dad that he had a job back in Illinois." Years earlier the boys had been sent to Chicago as partial settlement for burning the school.

"Dad's uncles lived there. They operated legitimate (so far as the authorities knew) successful businesses. So, the court here decided that the environment in a far-away state was better. It sort of worked for several years." Thinking ahead of Forrest, I thought: nurture, worldview, blood, whatever, has a way of catching up, governing you might say. According to Forrest, they had come back to Kentucky after a few years, to the old home, the trough, to new-found buddies with similar interests. Illinois officials had been moving in on the auto chop-shop where they worked at the time. Ace was now going back to Chicago. Kentucky's legal system, too, had got hot.

"'Pops,' Ace said on that last visit, 'If you can front me ninety-five hundred dollars, I can buy me a car to drive back to Illinois, and then to work. You won't believe what a deal I've worked out with a buddy up there. He has a used car dealership. He needs somebody to travel to the car auctions and buy for him—just my kind of work. He is going to pay me a grand a week. Can you believe that?'

"In earlier times Dad's answer would likely have been, 'no, I can't and I don't'." But a sick old father who has recently made a profession of faith in Christ and been Baptized in his kitchen begins to look for the best in people. That was the situation during Ace's last visit.

"Dad handed him the money in crisp greenbacks."

"Dad was drifting in and out of sleep during Ace's most recent visit." Forrest looked past me, a sad look, I thought. "Ace told Dad that 'the job fell through after a couple of months.'" His friend had changed the vin number on several cars—complicating licensure, insurance and ownership. "Funny how an old Dad can be fooled, ain't it?" Forrest, changing his demeanor completely, shook his head as he finished this report on Ace's most recent visit but didn't reveal Ace's request.

"Ain't a bit different with Duce." Forrest continued, filling me in on the second boy's line. "'Hey, old Bone Head, I've come to see you.' Dad was dozing when Duce entered the house. Even awake, he was in a stupor from the cancer medicine, but Duce's entry, and greeting, brought him around. He weakly smiled and invited his boy to come near his chair. They had a brief back and forth about Dad's health, Duce's current living arrangements, work, and love-life, but got around to the usual request. Duce needed money—fifteen thousand dollars to be exact. 'Pap, I've got a temporary problem.' Dad, sick as he was, knew Duce likely had money problems or he wouldn't be there.

"Dad found it impossible to turn either of the boys away. He didn't have much time left, and he knew it. He had the money he'd hidden from the insurance scam. Giving the boys just one more chance (even though that one more had already turned out to be several) might be the last they'd need and the last he could provide; just one more chance, and Ace or Duce might find themselves, see that the world had more to offer than what they had settled for. You see, Caleb, Dad felt the boys needed an opportunity, that they might get smart."

It was hard for Grifton to believe that his own blood knew so little about getting by in the world. Other than the insurance scam which had netted him millions, he had no legal issues. His gambling, drug deals, jewelry supply had been a profession, usually managed illegally, but always professionally.

Forrest straightened his shirt collar and continued to quote Duce. "'Pap, some of the boys are after me. I screwed up on a deal. The goods disappeared. I'm left owing thirty grand.'" Forrest looked at me as if to say, see what I mean about the money. "'Fifteen is all I've got. These fellows are from Chicago. They mean to have their money tonight.' "Duce's face was red. He was breathing hard as he said the last. Dad handed over the money in cash." Forrest shook his head. "Dad knew in reason that the problem involved drugs." Forrest grimaced as he said drugs.

"Duce gave him a gentle knuckle bump on the head and said, 'Bye, old Bone Head,' then strolled out the door. Dad took two pills and drifted back to sleep."

I wanted to finish Forrest's story, but did so only in my mind. Possibly Grifton dreamed about two ten-year old boys running through the back yards in the neighborhood, overturning swing sets, breaking flower pots, riding down fences, throwing a neighbor's June apples at other boys. Fathers see a lot. Much is overlooked, thinking, "Ah, they'll grow out of it. Little scrappers are mischievous". Forrest had graphically flushed out some of the boys' actions during Grifton's last years. I told him so and thanked him. One more rumor was nagging me. It involved Georgia Bell or Peachy as she was known—Grifton's step-daughter.

FRED WINKLER EVANGILIZING

Next to find Georgia Bell Davis but first things first. I stopped at the pump, at the local Chevron station, the same place where Grifton gave me the assignment regarding his boys. The station is a combination full-service station, a light and heavy-duty garage, and auto recovery center. It is crowded for parking but has a long bench along the front backed up to the plate-glass window.

Seated on the bench this morning are three men—Elmer Sigmon, Amos Moon, and Knot Head. Fred Winkler, standing facing them, is proclaiming something. The same McDonalds coffee club, the same friends of W. H. I stopped and listened, as the attendant fueled my car and moved it out of the way of the pumps. It's interesting how a group of men, young and old, will congregate around a smelly coal fired stove, or a camp fire on a lonely hillside enduring toasted fronts and cold backs and dodging dog droppings. Today, it's to sit and smell gasoline, diesel fumes, and gear-grease at their favorite station. Another group may well be in a dusty barn alleyway breathing fumes from cow or hog dung. They're pretty much all the same, considering cleanliness a home thing, a woman/family thing.

I picked up on the conversation this morning as Fred said, "Boys, I'll tell you what. You ain't never seen anything like it. Old big Albert Garland jumped up. He'll probably weigh two-fifty. Anyway, he took after Bumgardner, a little feller. I forget his first name. He works out of the county. Garland was going to escort Bumgardner outside and challenge him to something. Well, a couple of women got in front of big Albert blocking his passage. Little Bumgardner stopped at the exit, beside the piano, and wiggled his forefinger inviting Garland outside. Bumgardner's game. Now ain't that a sight, right in the First Baptist Church?"

"What was going on?" Knot Head was bouncing on his part of the bench, eager to get the details. Another thing about men. Most of them like to hear about a good fight, especially if the underdog wins. This encounter led to no fist-a-cuffs though.

"I'll tell you what happened," Fred continued. "We was having a business meeting, going to call an interim pastor to replace the Calvinist we'd just turned out. The Calvinists were organized this time. They had sixty-two votes. We had forty-one. Garland voted with the Calvinists. Bumgardner against."

"Sounds to me like that ended it then." Amos said this as he pulled his tobacco twist from his pocket. Facts often defy reason, however. Winners may shout and clap, but losers, even if they smile, are secretly gritting their teeth and considering their next step. This is true with most any group—political voters, shareholders, family discussions.

"Actually, no. There are too many extenuating circumstances." Fred had trouble with ex-tin-u-a-ting but finally got it out.

Elmer Sigmon who seldom said much at the gatherings spoke up from the end of the bench. Heads turned to see what he had to say. "I heard that old Aunt Em Crothers said she'd like to have seen little Bumgardner wipe a couple of stripes off the parking lot with big Garland. The bench was now shaking, somewhat dangerously considering the weight. Knot Head was stamping his feet and laughing.

Knot Head regained his composure first. Thinking of something he had heard down at the post office earlier in the morning. It needed to be reported. "They're saying that Mrs. Abby Murphy advised her old man before the business meeting that 'if trouble breaks out, pick somebody about your size. Don't tackle some long armed, big fisted man and get yourself crippled.'" Again, the bench shook with laughter.

Fred didn't consider it a laughing matter and fearing losing control of his report bellowed back in. "You men don't understand. We're talking about Calvinism, the reformed kind where the preacher is the boss, little children are doomed to hell, women have to keep in their place." Fred's hands were shaking by this time, he wiped sweat from his forehead, customers were gawking trying to make out what the clamor was about.

I went on into the station to get my credit card run. I was thinking as I went about the first Church, and the charge given to the disciples about taking the message to all people, to all nations. The in-fighting seems to hamper this. Too much energy is lost. I thought of Paul's letters to the early churches—his attempts to settle squabbles, Mark's dissent with Paul, the reformation fight, the Church's stance on earth rotation, whether it was round, the argument about infant baptism. The list goes on. Men are going to disagree period, I reckon. I remembered the theory put forth by some clergyman as reported by Trollope in his book, *Barchester Towers,* that "theological dissent is healthy". I handed my card to the clerk. The mental conflict faded.

On my way out, Amos Moon had control of the discussion. "There is no doubt in my mind and the Bible supports this, you have to be baptized to get to heaven. Fred, your Baptist meeting sounds more like a Democrat party precinct meeting."

Knot Head interrupted. "I'll tell you this, you fellers had better be thinking about end times, the beast, the tribulation. I heard my preacher say that others overlook the main point arguing about something that may or may not be biblical. The beast is biblical. Some say his mark is on the social security card we are made to carry. This modern bunch now says it's in a little chip or something that the government wants ever body to have stuck under their skin or on their forehead, I'm told." The other men shuffled and looked at their grease-spot on the concrete.

Fred, determined to get the last word, interjected, "The fellow the congregation steam-rolled in as interim pastor lied. He said he didn't even know what Calvinism was, and that, no, he wasn't a Calvinist. One of the members had a copy of his writings from his seminary days which was written in defense of Calvinism. Now what you say to that?" All agreed that they couldn't support a lying preacher. I nodded to each of the revelers and left.

Driving away from the station I considered what effect W. H.'s presence might have had on the discussion. I would love to have heard his input; however, his rambling monologue probably would have taken them far afield stifling the various viewpoints.

I need to get back on task—find the real Grifton, locate Georgia Bell 'Peachy' Davis, Grifton's step-daughter, born to the murdered wife. The rumors I've heard are not pretty. I decided to stop by the courthouse and see the County Clerk. She likely had an address on a car registration or something—giving me Peachy's location.

"Why, Mr. Grant, haven't you heard? They found Peachy down on Foggy Branch early last week, dead from an overdose, they said. She was just sitting in a car, dead." The clerk folded her hands to her breast as she said this.

I said, "No, I hadn't heard, I'm so sorry."

Life is short when viewed at my age, so full of worthy, exciting moments. Ending it prematurely, cutting short our allotted days, to miss blooms of springs, fall frosts, white snows of winter, blue, yellow, crystal reflecting from early morning dews discomposes me. An overdose on dangerous recreational drugs is suicide to my mind. Peachy's demise is so sad, doubly tragic when coupled with rumors I'd heard.

"I'm sorry, too, Mr. Grant, but not surprised. She's been troubled nearly all her adult life."

I should have inquired further, but people were bunching up behind me to see the Clerk. So, I thanked her and headed for my car. The courthouse sits across the street from the County Detention Center—which I had to pass on my way. On benches near the front door an assortment of individuals sat, some listening. Others were standing, smoking, throwing their hands first one way then another explaining their reason for being there, or telling a funny story related to someone inside behind the bars, the locked doors.

A teenage girl was staring, not at me. She appeared to see something that others could not. Her eyes, her sagging posture suggested that the vision was not pleasant. A grandmotherly lady sat with her hands clasp across her lap holding her purse, maybe protecting bail money. People like these, caught up in the cycle of family incarceration, gather daily awaiting visiting hours for those locked away. Such congregating is, more times than not, recurring. Peachy was not alone as a user. Neither is she alone as a fatal victim. I try to focus my thoughts, to better understand Peachy, to better understand Grifton, to better understand the mess that exists just below the cloud that I'm looking under. Many people float up through that cloud and go on to greatness, that's the beauty of our society, of the resilience of the human spirit. Our hope is that more float up and fewer slide down. The cloud hiding wretched living has always existed in every society. Individuals above that cloud are biblically commanded to reach down to lift others up. However, the number down there is growing. With Peachy gone there is one fewer to lift.

During the warm months a new group of back-packers saunter along our rural small-town streets: idle all day, gathering in groups to talk and smoke; at night they sleep in the bushes, move into vacant homes (without permission); others sleep in small tents on the outskirts. Some carry children. The group moves on after about a month making room for still another group. Amos Moon said to me once, "I've seen some delivered in an unmarked van, apparently private".

I don't remember who was with Amos during our discussion, maybe his brother-in-law. Anyway, he entered the discussion, or rather took it over. "Nobody seems to know who co-ordinates these transients' movements, who secures and manages their checks. No obvious local connections develop. They just move through— unproductive individuals on the lam, not on vacation. Instead they're more like the rail riders of the 1930's, except these moderns have government checks and eat at local hamburger stands. If they receive any training or job counseling it's not obvious."

Amos' facial expression was indicating wholehearted agreement as he interrupted. "Everybody needs to sleep somewhere, moving these groups around away from bad neighborhoods may be what they are trying to do. But, I agree, these people need training, counseling, work experiences."

My mind goes back to Peachy. We're better than this. Peachy's life was worth something. She began with such promise; didn't end as a transient back-packer but lost just the same.

GEORGIA BELL "PEACHY" DAVIS

After learning of Peachy's death I focused on investigating her high school days for a start and called on my teacher friend, Alma Farmer. I was sure she had taught at the high school long enough to have known Peachy as a student. While my wife and I often visit Alma, today I was seeing her differently—as a teacher. She's one of those people who may have changed over the years, but her demeanor is such that you still see her as she was twenty or thirty years earlier. She doesn't just smile. Her entire face is a smile. She's a bit pudgy. Her glasses are thick. Her brown hair shows signs of needing coloring. Her flats make her seem shorter that she is, but there is a caring nuance about her. It's neither young or old, just pleasant.

I explained to Alma the reason for my visit. Reviewing Peachy's tragic end, and the drug epidemic in our county took some time.

"Yes, Caleb, I remember Georgia Bell well. In fact, she has been one of my greatest disappointments." Alma looked at the far wall in her small, well-ordered living room as she said this. Her disappointment was obvious—in her eyes, her stance.

"May I inquire as to your disappointment, Alma?" I hardly knew how to address this without seeming gossipy even though I had explained my mission before we began.

"Georgia Bell was one of the most intelligent students I ever had in class. She was beautiful, outgoing, active in more clubs and school events than seemed possible. Caleb, she was one of those children who had everything. College, grad school, the world was open for her. Scholarships, community support, she had it all." Alma turned to a nearby table, retrieved a tissue, removed her glasses and dabbed at her eyes.

"I'm sorry, Caleb, but understand, I let her slip through the cracks. I had her in freshman English, then in AP classes for nearly three years. One gets attached, you see." I nodded, but the teacher-student bond was something I'd never experienced, so my actual seeing was questionable. I had experienced a loss when boys who had helped me on the farm went off to college, the army or better jobs. They were moving on up though. This was different. Peachy stumbled to a new level. She had moved to the shadows, present but invisible, just below that cloud, hidden, yet in sight.

Alma walked me to the door and again had more to say. Such discussions with such people are hard to close. "Even her eighth-grade test scores, her high school work—her speeches, her essays were so impressive. She left school without graduating, just faded out of sight. That was her final year, second semester, too. I tried to visit her, to call her, to make contact, but failed. I wept many a tear over that child."

As I stepped to the porch: "There is one thing. Something happened when Peachy was in elementary school that you might wish to pursue."

"I certainly will," I said before she had finished.

"I don't have the details, but word was that it was bad." Alma continued to dab first one eye then the other.

I admired Alma and wanted to offer comforting words, but merely patted her on the hand before excusing myself. Dedication, feelings like those Alma exemplify are rewarding to see. But what can one say to relieve another's apparent unfounded guilt?

I went home to Mandy not thinking about Grifton or the boys, but about the tragedy of Peachy's life. Mandy, has a way of ordering things and maintaining forward motion in most situations.

"Go see Wanda Fraley, Caleb. She has been over at the elementary school forever. If anybody can help you with the Peachy issue, I'm betting it's her." At that Mandy speed dialed a number. After their discussing DAR duties, and various other interests, an appointment was made for me to meet Wanda the following morning. Mandy just told her that I was interested in a school related issue.

On my way to meet Wanda I was asking myself questions, unanswerable questions. Why would a young girl with such potential sink so far so fast? Why would a young healthy person overdose? Was she taking illicit drugs? What happens in the mind when a capable beautiful person decides that the only alternative is a drug-induced stupor? Could she have gotten on the drugs accidentally a result of a misused prescription? Was the last dose a dangerously laced street drug? Was it peer pressure? Did something so traumatic happen back in her early life that affected her behavior as an adolescent and carry over into young adulthood? I had read about trauma affecting schoolwork, even learning ability. Terrible physical abuse of a toddler. Parental violence. Neglect to the point of no bonding with an adult. Sexual abuse. The list is long. Treatment is difficult, especially if the child experiences multiple traumas.

I settled on exploring Peachy's drug use as related to trauma since the rumors, including Alma's last suggestion, pointed to something unmentionable. I arrived at Wanda's house early and rang the doorbell fearful that she might not be up and around.

"Come right in. So, you are Mr. Grant. I've heard a lot about you from your dear wife, Mandy. I love that woman. She and I joined the DAR together. Did you know that?" I did know that and quickly realized that Wanda was the person I needed to see, that is, if she remembered Peachy. Wanda is apparently one of those eager to talk early-risers. Generally, I find them quite pleasant.

"Ms. Wanda, I appreciate your seeing me on such short notice. Mandy explained to you that I am seeking information on an elementary school child that you possibly had in class several years ago or that you possibly knew when she was at your school."

"No, she didn't explain your mission just that it was school related. I'll certainly help if I can." I briefly explained my Grifton mission and delved in.

"Ms. Wanda do you remember a little fifth grader, I think she was in fifth grade, by the name of Georgia Bell Davis, Grifton Davis's step-daughter?"

"Little Peachy, poor little darling. Yes, I remember her, taught reading to fifth graders at that time. We taught in blocks, you see, three teachers for each of the fifth and sixth grade classes. They've changed that all around now." Wanda was about to get me off mission. "Ms. Wanda, why did you say poor little darling when I mentioned Peachy?" Her opening remarks indicated that Mandy had steered me to the right person.

"Well, Mr. Grant, I hardly know where to start. The report I'm about to give you came to no resolution, and subsequently was handled as a gross misunderstanding. Personally, I was never satisfied with the outcome. But there is just so much a teacher can do. Of course, you realize that?" I said yes and asked her to take me through the specifics.

"It started on the playground with Peachy telling her playmates a horrendous story of something that happened the previous night." With that Wanda stopped, likely looking for words appropriate to share with a strange man. She turned her head toward the dining room behind her.

"Mr. Grant, I'm sorry. My manners have lapsed, I fear. Would you like a cup of coffee? I have it made. Let's sit at the dining room table where we can be comfortable. Your Mandy practices proper manners, I'm sure." With that Wanda smiled, rose from her wingback chair and beckoned me to follow. Wanda was obviously anxious. Concern for Mandy's reaction to manners I thought substituted for

Wanda's unease in discussing a delicate subject with Mandy's husband.

Once our coffee was properly creamed, Wanda folded her hands before her on the table and began. "Little Peachy described a sexual encounter that happened the previous night. She gave the children details and, of course, one of the children, big-eyed, reported specifics to the teacher—who happened to be me. There is always one who tells all, you know. What inappropriate was said at the water fountain, who dropped a wrapper on the playground, who lost their pencil. I can't for the life of me remember the child's name who gave the report." The child's report about Peachy tracked the coffee-shop rumor that Peachy had suffered sexual abuse as a child. So, I asked Wanda what she did next.

"I called Mrs. Deaver, one of the other fifth grade teachers and asked her to take the children to the gym. Then I called Mr. Maupin, the principal, on his intercom asking him to please come down to my classroom." Elementary school principals are usually glad to get away from the office. However, Mr. Maupin had no idea what he was about to hear.

"'Yes indeedy, Ms. Wanda', he said and came right on down."

"'Oh my. Oh, my goodness!' After hearing the story, Mr. Maupin walked the isle in front of my desk, wringing his hands, shaking his head side to side, and seeming to get smaller with each turn. 'What are we to do, Ms. Wanda?' Mr. Maupin organized to the smallest detail before school started each year. The school then pretty much ran itself. We had very dedicated teachers." Wanda looked at me for confirmation, or some comment.

"I'm certain of that," I said, speaking of the dedication of teachers in general. Wanda sipped her coffee and straightened the napkin beside her cup.

I asked what she did next?

"I explained to Mr. Maupin that we were required to call social services and that they must investigate and report their findings to proper authorities." I asked about Maupin's response.

"'Oh, yes, yes! Ms. Wanda, of course you are right. But what will happen to little Peachy, to us? Oh my. Oh my!'" Wanda raised her hands from the table as she reported this. "Mr. Maupin continued to walk and moan. He was a slight man, with thinning gray hair, generally dressed in a black suit and red tie. He was extremely shy of any sort of controversy. We teachers were to man the front line, always seeing that problems never rose to his level." Wanda moved on. "Two social workers came. The story was repeated by little Peachy. Each worker took her aside for an interview. They concluded that the story required further investigation and scheduled a home visit for that evening. I think the county attorney was involved at that point, or maybe the local police, I'm not sure. We heard nothing till the next morning when Mrs. Davis, Peachy's mother brought her to the Principal's office. I was called in. The mother, cool as a spring breeze, explained that Peachy had a vivid imagination, that the story was totally fabricated, had Peachy recant and apologize to Mr. Maupin and to me. I never saw the social workers again. Peachy was moved over to the Christian school across town."

A bit shaken I thanked Wanda and left the house. The entire scenario from start to finish was predicated on rumor, and a child's recanted story. Along with Wanda, I had doubts about the investigation, about the mother's role. Peachy's mother left Grifton shortly thereafter and was later found murdered in a rooming house in St. Louis. What's baffling is that Peachy, along with a brother, were left in Grifton's care. While facts are not available to substantiate it, Peachy's overdose, in my mind, suffices as circumstantial evidence of childhood trauma.

My goal is evolving. Grifton's original request has competition. I now believe the boys need to understand and adapt a degree of selflessness if they're to step off the trail toward personal self-destruction. Obviously, an ungoverned existence has been their mantra, life by unimpeded self-fulfillment, their goal. I realize this new concern, this new objective, to right their thinking is likely beyond my reach, yet I feel obliged to try.

PEACHY AND DEL—SOMETHING BIG

When I arrived home from the meeting with Wanda, Mandy had left a note saying she had gone shopping and to the movies with her sister, Eunice, and expected to be home late; that my lunch was in the oven, that she had a bit of news that might interest me, and that a University of Kentucky basketball game is on TV at eight o'clock. I was interested in all three—food, news, basketball. As I opened the oven the smell of lemon baked chicken, rolls, and mashed potatoes briefly replaced my thoughts about Peachy. Mandy's news interested me. I was sure it wasn't TV news. She seldom watches. Political news of late upsets her. It wasn't an emergency. She went off shopping and for entertainment. Her knowing up close my obsession with the Grifton search, I decided the news related to that.

It was the following morning before Mandy and I talked. I was sleeping soundly when she arrived home that night, well after our usual bed time. Responding to Mandy's note of the day before, I forgot to thank her for the supper. Instead I reported that I went to sleep during the game and didn't know who won, then quickly skipped to her news for me.

"Well," Mandy said, "Alma called me while you were at Wanda's yesterday and told me a little story about Peachy and her brother, Del." I had never heard of Del. Mandy placed grits, eggs, and bacon on the table before saying anything else. I sipped my coffee, noticed Mandy's red house-coat belted tight around her still small waist and her matching shoes, but then remembered that we're in our mid-seventies.

"Yes?" I said, as she took her chair across from me.

"This is just rumor. Alma inquired around with teacher friends after you left the other day. It seems that Peachy, hearing of Grifton's travels, his casino gambling, staying in lavish hotels, traveling with the who-is-who in the high roller crowd decided she and Del might enjoy a turn."

The phone rang and Mandy answered it in the kitchen. It was Eunice. Mandy's excitement was evident. The discussion went back and forth replaying various scenes from the previous night's movie, then moving on to the shopping purchases. Each "fit perfectly". I was unable to discern whether she was talking about items for the house or an outfit. The call may have lasted less than five minutes, but seemed more like an hour as I was eager to hear about Peachy and Del.

Mandy looked a little embarrassed when she returned to the table; "You know how it is with Eunice and me. We must share, rehash after we've been together. Where was I? Oh, yes, I remember, I was telling about Peachy and Del's plans for the high life. Alma told me that Peachy was probably fifteen years old. She described Grifton's travels, his big winnings, meeting high-rollers in Vegas, Cincinnati, Memphis and a dozen other cities to Del. To the children Grifton's stories were intriguing, daring, romantic, especially to fifteen-year-old Peachy. All grown up she decided she and Del might flourish in such an atmosphere."

Mandy's story, actually Alma's and her friend's story added a new chapter to Peachy's life. A girl's dream to sparkle, to make a show; a boy's dream to demonstrate his manhood can take many a course. What the two heard at home, saw played out pointed to sparkling lights, expansive hotel suites, far-away places, lots of money. No doubt Peachy and Del often discussed someday living that life. A local plumber reported seeing Grifton's house set up with a complete casino operation—roulette, gaming tables, slot machines—arranged to accommodate fifty or more people. This, the plumber had repeated down at the Chevron Station. The children likely saw the flashy set-up. Further, Grifton often returned from a weekend of gambling, his briefcase filled with cash, jewelry, and telling stories of bodyguards posted near players.

Bar-room gossip about Grifton snatching a man by his tie as he passed Grifton's table was likely heard by the children. Grifton supposedly pulled the man close, demanded settlement on an IOU accompanied by a threat of having him killed. The drama, the excitement, the winning was no doubt stamped in the children's minds. Mandy said the children had slipped away from school after first period on a Monday. This was a day of recovery for Grifton following a gambling weekend. They returned home and slipped in through Peachy's bedroom window. As Del hunkered at the bottom of the stairs Peachy quietly made her way up to Grifton's bedroom as the story goes. It was almost ten a.m., but Grifton was still out, snoring loudly. "I bet that room smelled of aftershave, women's perfume, alcohol from three-day worn clothing scattered around the bed." Mandy interjected this, then rolled her eyes.

Mandy also said that "Peachy later told authorities and friends about rifling Grifton's trousers, sliding her hand into each front pocket carefully lest keys or change rattled, until she felt his roll with the rubber band around it, and retrieving it. Holding the money roll against her breast until she rejoined Del, she handed it to him. motioning that he was to put it in his pocket.

"Talk was that the rest of the day was spent wandering backstreets, eating nabs, and potato chips, and planning. When school was out the two were sitting on Alvin Colby's front porch. Peachy knew that Alvin traveled to Corbin each afternoon to pick up his father after work. Alvin had made the trip twice daily since his father lost his driving privileges." Mandy examined her napkin. "You know Caleb, teenagers have talking relationships. Life events are shared with others who have personal experiences that aren't widely discussed. Peachy's and Alvin's frequent encounters since grade school, I'm betting, was such."

"I agree. How did they get out of town?"

"According to Alma, they concocted a plan to ride with Alvin to Corbin, catch a bus from there to Lexington, a taxi on to the airport, and board a plane to Vegas as they now referred to the Nevada city.

"You might say the rest is history; however, complications arose according to Alma," Mandy said. "Early that evening the two approached the Blue Grass Field's Delta ticket counter and ordered tickets to Vegas. They had no baggage, no carry-on, and were paying in cash, mostly one hundred-dollar bills. No matter that their shoulders were squared, that they were using their most grownup voices something just didn't seem right. They had no identification. The sales clerk excused herself and with her back to them phoned her supervisor." Shifting her weight in the chair, Mandy scratched her forearm.

Further reports reveal that moments later the children were seated in a small cubicle down the hall from the ticket counter in discussion with the supervisor, a smiling middle-aged lady with considerable airport experience. She gently drew out their story, mostly factual. Security was called, Peachy and Del were escorted to an office where after further questioning an officer phoned Grifton.

It was nearly two p.m. before Grifton stirred from his post-gambling sleep, to immediately discover his money gone. Pondering, he gathered pieces of clothing from around his bed. Who knew? Who would dare? These thoughts continued until late in the day. The phone call actually relieved him, just a little family mix-up—part of growing up. Grifton picked the two up and the three ate dinner at a private club in downtown Lexington.

Peachy and Del may not have been aware of a previous theft. Grifton had responded much differently. The youngsters had likely seen the long automatic gun stored under Grifton's bed. Grifton often publicized this to special acquaintances. The previous theft involved drugs. Friends of Grifton visited the trailer of the daredevil who violated his property. Using the same under his bed weapon, they riddled the home shattering every window along one whole side. Luckily no one was there. The message was delivered, however, just the same.

DEL ESCAPES

Now to find Del, the brother I'd just recently heard of, another step-child of Grifton's; unable to reach Forrest, the most likely resource, I began fishing for a way to find Del. Since learning of his existence, his connection with the Las Vegas caper, his close connection with Peachy, I decided that he too offered promise of pertinent Grifton information.

Del's high school principal, Mr. Godfrey, was my initial contact. "It's very nice of you to take time out of your busy schedule to see me," I said.

"Sure thing Mr. Grant." Mr. Godfrey was looking over my shoulder as he cinched my hand, his hand feeling at least twice as large. He was watching a group of boys near the fence across the school yard. "You cannot believe how much time is spent watching that crew." Godfrey gestured toward the boys. Seeing my puzzled expression, he continued. "Drugs, drugs!" The words were spat out. He then explained that dealers drove their automobiles near the fence and made sales virtually in view of the staff, but not today. Godfrey was on duty. A man to be respected, Godfrey had the build of a major league football player; the appearance of a drill sergeant, crewcut hair, wearing University of Kentucky sweats; someone you might expect to see in a sports bar, definitely not as principal of the county high school.

I told him of my mission to locate a former student. He led me inside the building, past the athletic trophy cases, to a small office next to the gymnasium entrance. "I remember Del," he said, "long blond hair, down to here," He pointed to his shoulder, and resumed, "didn't graduate, transferred out west someplace during his junior year." I asked if he knew anything about his whereabouts now. He shook his head. Then seeming to think of something, he asked me to come with him to the school library. We walked briskly down a long hallway, past students walking, laughing, gouging as they made their way to first period classes. We took a stairway up to a second floor, him taking the stairs in a jog, me huffing several steps behind.

Once in the library stacks he removed a school yearbook from an earlier decade and began scanning. "Ah, this is what I was looking for," he said, and leafed through the book. "Here he is." He pointed to a picture in the junior year section. Apparently Del didn't leave until later in the year. Del was pictured with the band, with the football team, and a single snapshot on a page with other classmates. Godfrey was correct. Del had long blond hair, piercing eyes, and was wearing a fatigue jacket. "Doesn't look anything like Grifton, you see."

He looked at me as if to say, luckily, he didn't have any Davis blood. "Didn't give us any trouble. Turned out to be a pretty good student, as I remember. He came to us with a weak grade average, however. Something about his mother being murdered so the school psychologist told me."

I said, "Mr. Godfrey you have a remarkable gift to recall all this about a student from that many years back."

"I try to know our students. Of course, Del was more memorable than most, his academic record on entry, the time staff committed trying to bring him around. I got him interested in playing football, that might have helped. We also had an outstanding band teacher. He mentored Del."

I asked Godfrey how this information might assist in the search for the boy. He flipped over a couple of pages and pointed to another boy with long black curls also down to his shoulders and dressed in a similar fatigue coat. "They were best friends. Cody Black, he still lives somewhere in the county. I see him at various school events." He glanced up at me as if obviously this might help.

"You think they're still in touch," I asked.

He nodded. "It's a start." He replaced the yearbook.

I thanked Godfrey at the front door, after noting the lunchroom smells—bread baking, veggies boiling, hamburger grilling, and spices suitable for lunchroom cooking. Our discussion hadn't provided a major breakthrough, but at least I had a lead.

The local phonebook was no help in locating Cody. Many people now using cell phones have cancelled their landlines. I decided to go to the internet. Cody's address came up, eliminating another hurdle in this endless pursuit of Grifton. I'd been examining threads, each merely replaced by another thread. My hope is that these threads flush out enough to eventually stich a composite of Grifton. Cody without long curls, face more filled out, wearing a button-down dress shirt and khakis greeted me warmly on my arrival at his house. I explained my mission and thanked him for seeing me. Eager to get his take on his friend, I asked what he remembered about Del Davis.

"Gee," he said, "we were best friends, you know. I'll try and pick out some of our exploits. Maybe that will tell you something."

"Yes," I said, "but before I forget, my secondary interest is to find Del, so if you can help on that." He stopped me.

"Del and I had different interests from most boys beginning in grade school. Of course, we were band members, played football, and goofed around with the guys, but mostly we made movies using a super-eight-camera. We spent hours in my parent's basement filming science fiction movies. Usually the hero was somewhere in outer space struggling with evil forces, fierce monsters, hostile environments."

Cody looked at me, a certain longing in his eyes, remembering carefree days, good friends, I figured.

"We finally graduated to spelunking. Now that was a trip. Del was fearless. One time he dropped down in a sinkhole, a single rope circled under his arms, then looped around his butt. The rope was over fifty feet long and played out before he touched bottom. The opening spread out under a huge dome several feet down. He couldn't touch anything around him. Luckily, we had the rope tied to a tree." Cody spread his hands and sighed. "I like to never got him out of there, wouldn't have, in fact if one of the Collier boys hadn't decided to join us. It's a wonder, boys ever get grown, isn't it?" We both laughed in agreement. Inside I was cringing, visualizing the dark hole, the dome, the boy hanging in the middle of it, depending on a couple of teenagers to save him.

Cody snapped his fingers indicating a thought. "You said you wanted to find Del. I probably can help. You know how Facebook works, friends have friends who have friends. Anyway, Del and I made contact several years ago through Facebook and continue to communicate now and then. Let me pull him up on my phone." Cody scanned through what seemed to be hundreds of Facebook entries. "Yes!" he said. "Here's my old buddy." He held the phone before my face. Pictured was a nice looking blond man, his hair combed back, wearing a Steve Jobs tee shirt and denims.

Cody then proceeded to tell me what he knew about Del. Married ten years, he had two children, lived in Oakland, California. He and a couple of classmates from the University of California had started a dot com enterprise in one of their basements, something to do with robotics. The endeavor blossomed and all three became wealthy, according to Cody.

Del had come a long way. His start with Grifton certainly hadn't held him back. We often read about and talk about children's resilience. Del's background and apparent outcome is remarkable. Cody punched the phone several times and said, "Ah, here is his phone number."

I asked Cody if he and Del ever recount their childhood experiences. "Not much," he answered. "We have written a couple of times about the filming." I asked Cody if he ever visited Del's home when they were boys.

"No, Mr. Grant, I didn't." Cody leaned back slightly as though he'd just as soon not go into it.

I had to know why, however, and said, "But he was often at your house?"

"Yes, to tell you the truth, Mr. Grant, I wasn't allowed."

Oh? I said and leaned closer to Cody. "My parents didn't think it a fit house."

"Now that you are older, do you think they were right," I asked?

Cody pushed his phone into his pocket and did a little sidestep. "There were an awful lot of rumors." Cody turned, removed his phone from his pocket and placed it on the table behind him, bringing the discussion to a close, I assumed. I told him how much help he'd been and how I appreciated being invited into his home as he showed me to the door.

KNOT HEAD'S INFORMATION

"He sold that load of timber and it not even his." Driving home from Cody's house, I stopped at Walmart to pick up some notions for Mandy. Knot Head, presumably going home, was sauntering along the side walk as I pulled out of the store parking lot. I stopped and asked if he wanted a ride which he gladly accepted, reporting that his old truck wouldn't start that morning. Noting that I was looking at his Walmart bag, he explained that he'd bought a set of spark plugs.

"Ain't none of 'em any account no more." Knot Head shook the bag, "a little cheaper out here than over at the parts house though." Just to make conversation, I mentioned that I was gathering information on Grifton Davis. This caused Knot Head to eagerly begin a story about Grifton's dad. Before the printing press people got to talk, to transmit their stories, to pass on civilization. In this part of Kentucky, we still have people with little concern for the written word, other than examining their mail, or a sale flyer. Knot Head fits this description. His stories, mostly gossip, are not meant to educate or entertain. They're an opportunity to talk, to be heard. His kind leaves a conversation fully satisfied—he and so and so had had a good talk.

Knot Head looked over at me, his Adam's apple protruding and moving up and down, his John Deer cap pulled low in front and sitting on his ears and continued. "Sold them logs, he did. I never did hear Grifton's pap's name. They always just called him Happy. Anyway, Happy was walking out of the holler one Saturday morning, the ground was froze, a big frost on. He was wearing a little lite jump-jacket and Milt somebody, I can't call his last name, stopped his log truck and picked Happy up. Town was a right smart piece, you see. Milt had on a big load of logs taking them to the mill just the other side of town. Well, when he got to the

court house in town, he stopped to let Happy out. Happy said, 'I believe I'll just ride on over to the mill with you'."
Knot Head chuckled when he said this.

"You'll never believe this! When they got in the log yard, Happy asked to get out, said he'd go in and get Milt's check while he unloaded, save him a little time." Knot Head leaned closer and looked at me preparing for the punch line. "That rogue went in the office and told the clerk he had a load of logs outside and when he, the clerk, got the measurements from the checker just to make two checks, half to Milt and half to him. The clerk did too. Let me tell you something, Caleb, Happy was slick." Knot Head drew a face, his lips pursed, his forehead wrinkled, indicating he didn't approve of such.

I asked Knot Head what happened when Happy got back to the truck with Milt's half-pay for his week's work. "Ah, he looked at the check and said he thought he had a bigger load than that. Happy got out as they went back through town. He had him some extra spending money, Caleb. That's what he was after. But who would have thought of skinning a feller like that. I'd a been afraid to even if I's a notion, wouldn't you?"

By the time Knot Head finished the Happy story we were in front of his house. "Pull there in the yard," he said and pointed to a clear spot close to his truck. "I've got some more to tell about the Davis bunch if you got time." I didn't say it but I'd have spent all day if need be, since Knot Head had exactly the type information I was after.

I killed the motor and sat back. Knot Head began. "Uncle Houston, that's Daddy's uncle, use to come over on cold winter days when they couldn't get out and do anything. He and Daddy sat around the stove all day, talking old times. Now and then one of them put a block of coal in the stove. Smoke puffed out the door and settled on the ceiling. A good yard square was black as night above the stove. Both of 'em chewed. They spit in the ash bucket. Mommy said that was better than the floor." Knot grimaced at this.

"I's just a boy and Mommy wasn't too keen on me hearing ever thing they talked about either. Uncle Houston lived in the holler for several years, just down a little and across the creek from Happy. He was considerable older than Grifton. So, he saw Grifton from the time he's running around the yard naked until he's a great big boy, near a man." Knot Head shifted in the seat, straightened his leg the best he could, and began rubbing the calf. "Charlie-horse, you ever have them, Caleb?"

"Now and then," I acknowledged.

"Grifton got a hold of a goat somewhere. He put together a makeshift cart to ride on and broke the goat to pull it. Uncle Houston said that goat minded ever word Grifton said—almost like it understood talk. One time, Uncle Houston said he seen Grifton on that cart, the goat pulling it and running fast as it could down the track along the creek bank. The other boys was running along behind, actually they's riding stick horses, whooping like wild Indians, and pretending they's after the stage coach. They's a big rock right in the edge of the track, a boulder that had rolled off the hill in past years. It was taller than a man. When the goat passed the rock, the cart wheel hung and throwed Grifton against the rock, nearly killed him, Uncle Houston said. Did you ever notice that scar in Grifton's hairline above his left eye?"

"No," I said.

"I saw it many a time. That's exactly where that scar come from." Knot Head stopped to think and squinted his eyes. I asked how old Grifton was at the time of the cart wreck.

"Oh, I'm not sure, maybe eight or ten." I inquired whether his uncle reported anything about Grifton's teen years.

"I don't remember a lot. He did say all the boys worked. There was a bunch of them, you know, big stout fellers. Except Grifton managed to get by without getting dirty.

Happy'd buy a boundary of timber and use the boys and others to take it out. Uncle Houston helped some. Grifton maneuvered to make the half-day trip to the post office and store most days. He'd carry the drinking water from the spring. He'd walk to town for a file or whatever the crew needed. He didn't pull a crosscut or handle a cant hook though." Knot Head chuckled. "Happy paid up on Saturdays, and more times than not, engaged the crew in a crap game. On those gambling Saturday's, the crew often went home broke or nearly so. Uncle Houston said Happy never got him in one of them games. He'd been warned by his Pa."

"Sounds to me like Grifton turned out about like he was reared," I said. "Well in a way he did, and in a way, he didn't," Knot responded. "Happy never got out of the holler, away from the farm. He died in the log woods, in his seventies, if I remember right. By Ned, Grifton got out. The other boys did too. But Grifton made a splash. He went to Las Vegas. He gambled in several states. He built big houses, drove a Cadillac, dealt in fine diamonds. He had a gang of workhands, handled big money. Of course, he wound up going to the pen, but he didn't hurt nobody, did he, except the big insurance companies. The insurance companies hurt a lot more people than Grifton did." Knot Head looked at me for confirmation. Being polite, I gave a slight nod.

On my way home, re-running Knot Head's report in my mind, I was thankful for the information, and considering how to use it in Grifton's boys report.

Several days after the encounter with Knot Head, I received a call from him. One never knows who will assist along the way. Certainly, Knot Head had not been on my list. Turns out he had given our conversation some thought.

"Caleb, I been studying about mine and your talk about Grifton Davis," he said. "I been talking to my cousin, Irene, and she told me that her grandma on her mother's side was a school teacher. She teached down at the Gladiator School back in the thirties, maybe before."

"Is that right," I said? I had never heard of the Gladiator School. Knot Head explained that it was one of the one room schools that dotted the county until the nineteen fifties and was located over on the creek about a mile from his Uncle Houston's and the Davis's homes. Both families sent their children there at least for brief periods.

"Irene told me that the Davis boys was in her grandma's school." Knot Head raised his voice as he presented this information, pleased with himself that he was being helpful. "Irene heard her grandma tell her mommy that the Davis boys were clever, but reading, writing, and arithmetic was not high on their list. They just didn't care much for learning." Knot Head paused, organizing his thoughts for the rest of the report. "Irene's grandma said that Grifton just attended through third grade. He was naturally good at arithmetic though. He did problems with the sixth graders." That information fit with Forrest's report on Grifton's ability to figure sales in his head faster than merchants using their calculators. It also helped explain his proficiency in knowing the odds at the gaming table.

Knot Head laughed loudly, then added. "It was rough over on the creek in them days. Uncle Houston told Daddy that one of the Davis cousins come to a pie supper drunk once and shot into the heating stove with an old pistol. Broke the gathering up, too; people jumped out windows, crowded one another at the door, some of the children was forgot inside. I don't know if he was mad about somebody out-bidding him on his girl's pie or just being ornery." After completing this last tidbit, Knot Head said he'd better hang up. He'd promised a neighbor a load of fire wood. I thanked him and started to say goodbye.

Something had been on my mind from time to time, and impulsively I decided to ask Knot Head for clarification. I asked him if Knot Head was his real name. "No, no it's not,

Caleb, but if you inquired about me around the county by my real name, say you'se looking for me, nobody'd know who you was talking about." Knot Head laughed. "I got the Knot Head name from Uncle Houston when I was just a little tike. Mommy didn't like it a bit either. You know she finally got used to it though and started using it same as ever body else."

"Do you mind telling me what your real name is?"

"Not one bit. The only time it's used is on my driver's license and pension check though. It's Ulysses Turner. I'm glad it's not used, never did like it, took me forever, it seemed, to learn to spell Ulysses."

"Ulysses is a very strong name, Knot Head, a lot of history behind it," I said.

"You don't say." Knot Head had a lilt in his voice. In my mind I could see him squaring his shoulders and honing his diction. I said goodbye, but later felt guilty. Further name discussion was warranted if for no other reason it'd give Knot Head something to expound on with the coffee club. Grifton was still not speaking, but at least a picture of who he really was is developing. His spoken word regarding his sons is driving my quest though. The words were spoken years ago at the service station. Who knows, they may have just been words spoken for the audience. That thought leads me to further question the merit of my mission—a journey or a fool's errand, time spent either way.

Time for life often robs one of the life expected. Forty minutes from rising to sipping the last bit of milk from the cereal bowl. I didn't notice such until now. Inching slowly through early years to twenty, finding much later that it was a good, fun-filled twenty-seven percent of one's allotted years too swiftly passed. Bouncing through the twenties and thirties to find how little we know how little we've learned. Suddenly forty-five turns to fifty-five, skips to seventy-five. One has learned how to live at last, but the legs hinder. That may be where I am: writing a little for a weekly paper, and now spending years trying to understand a man who can no longer talk to me, trying to explain his life to men who likely don't care. I'm in too deep to quit, but I question sparing this time. Is this living? Maybe. Possibly it's about being occupied beyond the necessary.

FINDING DEL

Finding Del took more than a phone number from Cody; it took persistence and time. I called the number Cody gave me early morning, then at dinner time for several days. The answering machine was all I got; left a message giving my name, phone number, and address; didn't mention Grifton or Peachy. At eleven-forty p.m. on the third day, Del returned my call. Calling at that late hour, I assumed he'd forgotten the time difference. I was delighted when he identified himself even though it was late and interrupted *Longmire* on Netflix.

Del apologized for not returning my call earlier. He and the family had just returned from an Asian sales trip. His wife needed a vacation and the children an educational experience, he said. His accent was a mixture of Southeastern Kentucky and California, his voice soft, but businesslike.

"How may I help you Mr. Grant?" Answering his question over the phone with no preliminaries took me off guard. I didn't know whether to start with condolences regarding Peachy or the Grifton quest. Not personally knowing Peachy created complications; how to explain my concern for her. Mentioning Grifton first seemed calloused. So, I settled on Peachy and said I was sorry to hear about the death of his sister.

"Thank you, Mr. Grant. We hadn't been close for several years, but her loss has been hard, first our mother, now her. I have very little connection with Kentucky now. The step-siblings are older, you know. They were out of the house. I hardly knew them."

Del, what can you tell me about Grifton, about your childhood living with him, I asked, after briefly reviewing my reason for contacting him. "Actually, I had a lot of pain dealing with Mother's death, not knowing what really happened and depending on Grifton for emotional support.

Blocked. I suppose that's the best way to put it. For the most part I've blocked out those years. You know, I remember my school principal, the band teacher, Cody, that's about it."

"What was your and Peachy's relationship with Grifton like?" I asked.

"You might say, okay. Yeah, I guess it was. We had no other experience to make a comparison. He bought our clothes, fed and housed us, sent us to school. I wasn't close to him though. In fact, I never really trusted him. He was more of a shadow that filled our world, that is, when he was around. You probably already know, he traveled a lot. Peachy had more of a love-hate relationship with him, I think. She got me to help rob him once." Del chuckled as he spoke of the robbery. I asked if he and Peachy ever considered living elsewhere after their mother left.

"We often talked about running away, but there was no one nearby to run to. The aborted trip to Las Vegas was our only attempt. It was a lucky day for me when Uncle Harvie, Mother's uncle, brought me out here. Peachy was invited to come along. I have never understood her refusal."

"What was Peachy's hate relationship toward Grifton about?" I was uneasy about this question.

"I don't really know. He treated us both the same. We saw the gambling in the house, the jewelry sales, and sometimes there were creepy people, some wearing neck-braces. We tried to stay out of the way when he entertained those guys. Peachy was really smart, you know, and older too, maybe saw something I didn't."

I continued to probe. "Were you aware of the insurance scam?"

"Not really. Peachy and I often discussed the meetings, a mixture of family and others. These took place periodically. There were cryptic discussions, no gambling, alcohol, or food at those gatherings. Everybody seemed serious to me."

"Cryptic talk?" I wasn't sure what he meant.

"Places and people were mentioned without any flushing out. Doctor, accident, hospital exams—just words no context that we understood."

"So, were you suspicious."

"As I told you before, I didn't trust Grifton. This may be part of it, I guess."

I asked him how he accounted for his survival, his thriving while Peachy's life took such a hopeless turn.   I immediately regretted asking this. Del didn't hesitate though.

"My getting out of that environment probably saved my life. While I stayed above the fray, you might say, sooner or later, I think…" Del's voice got low and then quiet.

I grew skeptical as to getting anything new. Del's reply had a finality to it, but I continued the query. "Any memorable, redeeming quality about Grifton?"

Del's voice came back stronger, obviously revived:

"Grifton sent substantial sums of cash to a couple of charities each year. I know about those because Peachy addressed, boxed, and mailed them." Del went on to tell me that no letter accompanied the mailings. Each was sent registered with just a P.O. Box number as a return address. The mailings were always insured.

This information was new. I inquired about the charities and the amounts.

"I don't know about the amounts, but Peachy said the envelopes were stuffed full of big bills. Both charities provided services to children. I do recall that. Oh, and something else, he didn't punish Peachy and me for robbing him that time." Del chuckled again.

Del's voice got serious. "He did secure Peachy's bedroom windows."

"To prevent her sneaking out?" I quizzed?

"I'm not sure," he said.

"One other thing I remember. Peachy told me about something she saw once. Grifton brought several gamblers home for an extended game, had them park their cars elsewhere. He transported them in to prevent possible neighborhood suspicions. As the night progressed, a break was declared and Grifton put music on." Del's voice had a lilt in it as he continued.

"According to Peachy, there was a little pink-haired lady, old lady actually, from Cincinnati named Billie. She bantered Grifton to dance. The music was *Elvis' Jail House Rock.* Grifton took Billie up. Peachy said he was a dancing fool. They cavorted and the gamblers gathered in a circle, their hands up, bodies swaying, some shouting encouragement."

"That was a pretty feisty song for an old lady," I interjected.

"Raunchy is more like it," Del said. "She matched him move for move, the old lady's diamonds flashing, her skirt rising on certain turns revealing her panties. Grifton picked up the pace on every verse. Peachy said she was afraid the lady might have a heart attack any minute."

Del laughed loudly before starting again which I thought strange, as a life could have been at stake. "On the last verse Billie began unbuttoning her blouse."

"To disrobe, you think?" I too began to laugh and had to interrupt.

"Yeah, it was obvious. One of the women broke the circle and hugged her up to prevent a further display."

"Did that end the party?" I questioned.

"Oh, no. Billie moved toward the counter, slightly bent forward rolling her hands and wiggling her hips still in dance mode. She poured a jigger of whiskey, swallowed it down, threw her glass at the far wall, and returned to the table yelling, 'I'm dealing'."

Del paused. "You know when Billie died, she left her diamonds to Grifton. He gave one to Peachy. Worth a lot of money, Grifton said. Of course, it didn't do poor Peachy much good. I think she lost it or pawned it, more likely"

I heard someone yell, "hey Dad," in the background.

Del began talking fast, "Sorry, Caleb, I'm getting another call. I've enjoyed talking with you. It's good to hear from someone back East. Maybe I can come visit you someday." His voice slowed and lowered, "try and reclaim my boyhood even." I understood his sudden ring-off. A man who had just returned from an Asian trading venture likely had business to transact.

The cold-call hampered our communication somewhat, but Del's information was helpful. Grifton had been portrayed as a close-trading diamond salesman, a hard-nosed trucker, and a no-risk, calculating gambler. To learn from a reputable source that he was also a generous philanthropist puzzled me. We hear reports about a person, think that's him, that sums the guy up, then new information floats up which completely changes the trajectory of our thinking. Each of us has a story. Grandfather was hung as a horse thief, or made the charge up San Juan Hill, got his start as a moonshiner, or stood guard with Lincoln at Gettysburg. Grifton's story stands out, but not like any of those just mentioned. He is characterized sometimes as a terrible scoundrel, other time as a very caring fellow. Either description is dependent on the source. According to most, his good fails to mitigate his rumored evil—a personality proving difficult to reveal.

I was not sure where to turn after the Del queries. If they can be found, Ace and Duce are likely candidates. I also hope to get their full names. Information on them thus far reflects a Grifton personality gone sour, lodging deep under the cloud that's beneath polite, civil society. I've traveled under that cloud many times and always returned feeling guilty for having offered no hand up, or guilty for feeling dirty—results from investigative work versus missionary work, or philanthropic work, I suppose. I'm not talking about down and out people, I'm talking about people Poppa referred to as sorry.

A few days later, shopping at IGA offered more than a discount on gasoline. In the paper-goods isle I bumped my cart into a near full cart and said, "Excuse me," to a woman counting the rolls in a package of paper towels.

She said, "That's okay, Mr. Grant." I was pleasantly surprised to look around and see that it was Forrest Davis's wife. We inquired about each other's health and family members. I then took the opportunity to question her as to Ace's and Duce's real names. Mrs. Davis turned her head to the side, looked down and after a considerable pause, said, "Ace's name is Bedford, or something like that".

After Bedford Forrest, I surmised.

"Now, let me think. Oh yes, I do remember Duce's name. It's Robert Lee." She gave me a triumph look. I was not surprised at either name. "Come see us," she said, placed the towels back on the shelf and pushed off toward the meat counter.

ACE AND DUCE

William Harrison had previously reported that Ace and Duce were in jail; Ace here at home and Duce in Clark county. My search began locally. The deputy jailer welcomed me warmly, a plump lady, blond ponytail, gun and cuffs dangling over her wide hips. She smiled when asked about Ace. "Oh, he's gone, thank goodness. You talk about needy. I answered more calls from his cell than from any other ten inmates. He called me back there once, wanted me to rub his neck. These dudes get horny soon's they dry out, you know. I wasn't about to get suckered into that." She rolled her eyes up at me as if to say, bet you didn't think I'd tell that, did you? "Oh, and another thing, he tried to get me to go way down on 839 and get him one of their 'good hamburgers'. I told him, this wasn't a cab stand. Besides, I'm married." Asked if she knew where he might be located, she shook her head, the ponytail swishing side to side.

At the exit desk, I asked if inmate addresses were entered in the admissions reports. "Maybe." A little scared looking seventyish grey-lady, answered. Inquiring relative to Ace's home address, I was told that she didn't know if she was allowed to give it, then turned to the phone on her desk and dialed the jailer, I assumed. Turning back to me, "Who wants to know"?

"Caleb Grant."

I heard the jailer's response. "Yeah, give it to him," this delivered in a what-the-heck manner.

Just as I suspected, Ace's living situation was substandard plus. While not a falling-down trailer, it was a falling down house. The porch swayed toward the center. Planks were missing. The front door had a piece of plywood where the window once was; the outside knob missing, a tangle of battery cables and car parts lay across the entrance. I raised Ace after pounding several times. He opened the door wearing blue jeans with the knees showing, no shirt, hair tousled. "I's resting," he said, while raking his fingers through the frowsy hair. On closer examination, his begrimed jeans looked as though they'd stand-alone lest the open knees allowed unnatural bending. I wasn't invited into the house. We talked standing on the porch, my left leg bearing most of my weight due to the sway of the porch, as I made lame excuses for the visit.

I decided not to address Ace as Bedford. After preliminaries, the discussion turned to Grifton. I asked how he remembered his Dad now that he's grown and Grifton is gone.

"He was a captain, we use to call him goat-man, not to his face of course." Ace grinned as he stated this. Noting that a front tooth was missing, I pressed on, questioning Grifton's captain description, not the goat-man statement. Knot Head had covered that.

"Ah, he had more children than one of them old Mormons."

"How did your Mom handle that"? A dumb question but I wanted to hear his take on their relationship.

"She thought Grifton was the trick. Whatever he did was just great. Waited for him for years thinking to get married. I don't know what she wanted with him. He was old enough to be her grandpa." Ace became more serious. "Mom had a hard time, worked cleaning motel rooms. Duce's mom didn't have it any better. Dad gave both our mothers money, but in the early days drugs got most of it."

"What about you? How were you treated?"

"Alright, I guess." Ace kicked the battery cables out of the doorway. "He was gone most of the time. Me and Duce got sent out of state. Dad did help me a right smart before he died. Loaned me money. I never had to pay it back." Ace looked at me, his penetrating dark eyes expectant, ready for the next question. Over six feet tall, with Grifton's black wavy hair, fine featured nose and chin, Ace was good-looking, like his boyhood picture that his dad showed years ago. He needed dental work, thirty more pounds, and a good cleanup to actually merit the good-looking description.

My next question: "Can you tell me anything special you recall about Grifton?" Ace turned and looked through the door into the house as though the answer was inside. Turning back and grinning again, he replied.

"Well, he never beat me, nor mom either, as far as I know." Ace took a deep breath expanding his chest. "He'd a done well to beat me. I needed it." Ace stated the latter more as a badge of honor. "Another thing, me nor Duce neither one ever had to work. He made sure we had spending money, good clothes, bicycles, and later cars—even when we were living out there with our uncle. He brought me a near new Camaro when I got sixteen, Duce a nice Mustang. We raced them all over the country. Un-telling how many speeding tickets we got before the cars tore up." Ace clapped his hands, bent slightly, and laughed at this revelation.

What I said next just popped out without forethought. "Ace do you wish you'd taken a different path, done something else with your life?"

He didn't take offence, just kept smiling. "Yes, by hell I do. I wish I had had more women, gambled, built good houses, and traveled more. Do you think it is too late?" How to answer?

My mind went blank. "You know that describes Grifton's life don't you," I finally managed to croak out.

"Yeah," he said.

"But Grifton wound up in jail," I retorted not too pleasantly.

"Maybe he did, but he lived up till that time. Nobody told Dad what to do. He was a free man, happy too, got whatever he wanted, put more rings on more people's fingers than England's old King Henry. I think he was in England."

Somewhat frustrated and ready to leave, I asked about Duce. "That son-of-a-gun is in jail in Clark county or someplace like that. I got a call from him last Saturday, said he might be getting out the twelfth."

"Mind if I check back with you? I'd like to meet him," I replied.

"Come by later in the day on the twelfth. He'll want to nap after he gets here." Ace didn't inquire and I didn't offer any real reason for visiting.

Gripping the steering wheel as I left, realization hit: imposing our values on someone else, especially an adult is undoable, a fool-hearted exercise. Re-education takes time and effort. Even that may prove fruitless with Ace. My frustration boiling, I, not for the first time, considered W. H's. supposition about not being responsible for rearing these men. His conclusion rang truer with the Ace encounter.

That evening after explaining what a downer it had been to meet Ace, Mandy in her matter of fact way said, "what did you expect, a flower garden out front, a healthy wholesome looking young man watering the lawn, a sit-down snack with cloth napkins?" Reconsidering, she smiled and placed her hand on my shoulder. "You knew this wasn't going to be a feel-good exercise. Most people would have given up long before now."

She kissed me on top of my head and hurried off responding to the clothes dryer buzzer. Remembering that I hadn't cleaned the vent yesterday as asked, I followed her to assist in folding. One must be careful. The "bad eye, *the look*" is always just one forgotten promise away.

ROBERT LEE "DUCE

I dreaded Duce. Having heard the stories about his volatile personality wasn't encouraging. Having to encounter him on their territory—Ace's porch—didn't help. Slightly shorter than Ace, he made up for it in bulk. The jail food, exercise room, rest, whatever, had agreed with him. He looked healthy and strong. Beyond that, there was little to recommend him. Scraggly black beard extended down to his chest, rings in his nose and ears. A tank top revealed a snarling bear face tattoo on his left shoulder, his right shoulder decorated with the tail of a rattle snake. The snake itself coiled around his arm to the wrist where the head looked to be striking should he extend to shake hands or to deliver a punch. I introduced myself.

"Yeah, Ace told me about you, that you were talking about Dad, the old fart. He had it made, you know, like, he never had to get out and hustle day jobs like me."

"What do you do?"

"About anything—plumbing, electrical, roofing, raking leaves." Ace was looking over his shoulder and winked as though to say that's a bunch of bull.

"What do you most enjoy doing?" I asked?

Duce gave me a big smile, turned and presented Ace the same look. "Mostly I like to buy ten, sell five, take five, and buy ten more along with a burger and fries." He did a little dance step on the swayed porch demonstrating just how much he enjoyed that work. He then leaned against a very unstable looking porch post.

I was pretty much stumped. Each question was shadowed by the last answer. I turned toward the yard and commented on the motorcycle lying on its side. "Yeah, Ace is going to help me work on it," Duce said this as he rolled a cigarette. He used equipment unfamiliar to me in this exercise; a rectangular box maybe one by six inches forming a trough—this filled with loose tobacco which was pushed by a plunger into a pre-rolled paper. It produced a perfect smoke.

"A lot cheaper," he said as he lit up, and tapped his rear pocket as though to say, I know how to get by. Ace and Duce were not living off the grid, but they qualified as living on the cheap.

"I guess you've seen a lot traveling around on your cycle." I was struggling trying to get into Duce's mindset, his inner thoughts that governed his behavior.

"About everything 'cept a grey squirrel whup a coon." He grinned considering the response a good one. "I did see Dad repossess a car once. He called it repossess, actually he was collecting a gambling debt. The fellow moaned and begged, said he didn't have any other way to get to work. Dad pointed out that he should have thought of that before throwing the title down in the dice game. Dad was smart, tough too. He made money, gave that car to Mom."

Duce's eyes seemed to light up. "Once when I was riding bikes with a gang, well they weren't exactly a gang, we just hung out together, smoked a little pot, picked up a few odds and ends. There was one old tall scraggly-looking boy took a handkerchief with half dozen big taps, you know bolt taps, tied up in it and beat the shit out of four other bikers. I stayed out, didn't have no pot in that fight. You got to be careful, you know what I mean? Like somebody might coldcock you, and you not even know why." I said, I guess that's right, and waited to see what he might say next.

Ace spoke up, "Did you know Duce is getting his disability?"

"I haven't got it yet," Duce interrupted. "Getting it first of the month, I'm told; my lawyer is a hum-dinger. Got a right smart of back pay coming too; gonna buy me a big Dodge Hemi with an oversized exhaust. People will know old Davis is coming." Duce spewed this out. Then spit off the porch and ground his cigarette underfoot.

Both looked at me for comment, faces drawn with what I'd learned was the Davis grin, eyes squinted, head lowered. But my mind was occupied. I had known two hard-working men in their sixties, one bed-fast, the other hardly able to leave the house. One struggled for over two years to get his disability. The other's first check arrived a month after he passed away. Both had refused to get attorneys involved since the perk had been paid for, purchased during forty years of work. The application and appropriate medical documents, they thought, were sufficient.

"Is this permanent?" I finally continued the discussion. "Probably," Duce answered. "My back hurts terrible." He passed his hand across his lower back for emphasis. I had no specific reason to think fraud, but Duce's disability was not visible. Recently CBS reported on a Kentucky attorney practicing in Pike and Floyd counties, convicted for fraudulently filing disability claims in the amount of five hundred fifty million dollars; reportedly the most expensive social security disability fraud case in the nation. A doctor, a counselor, and a judge were implicated. The thought crossed my mind that Duce could be one of his cases. The doctor was paid six hundred thousand dollars for signing documents without examining the patient. This scam trumped Grifton's—carried out against one of the tightest regulated programs in the nation.

Ace laid his hand on my arm. "Mr. Grant, will you give us a ride downtown as you go? Duce needs to pick up his prescription." The Davis grin again.

Realizing that the discussion must be over, I said. "Yes". My goal to help these men overcome their rationalizing and justifying their behavior was looking more and more unachievable. *Antisocial personality disorder* comes to mind. I have read that this is both nature and nurture in origin, and very resistant to any treatment, certainly beyond my intervention.

HAVING GRIFTON THOUGHTS

Feeling stalled in my search and thinking nightly about Grifton instead of sleeping: is it possible that what I'd gathered was all there was to him? Was he now actually speaking to me? Before sleep, my mind rambled. Eventually Grifton's thinking, not my own, rose somewhere in my brain.

Ran around the yard naked as a boy. Had nothing but a goat cart for a toy. Goat and brothers for friends. Stank all the time. No tricycle, bicycle, or scooter. No basketball, football, or baseball. Did play stickball a few times. Happy put me to work soon as I could walk. Wanted me in the log woods. Never farmed. Mother worked like a slave. Happy lived by his wits, taught me how to gamble. Shuffled and re-shuffled cards, tossed and re-tossed dice till I was better than Happy and finally I was better than anybody. School was nothing. I beat all of them in arithmetic. Walked out of that hollow soon as I was big enough. Never looked back. Always had a woman from fifteen years old. Shoveled coal. Loaded the other fellow's truck. Saved earnings and winnings, bought my own truck. Got two more. Made a business hauling coal and melons. Learned about antiques and jewelry. No more coal dust and long rides. Bought and sold at a profit. Had gambling friends in funeral business. Good place to buy old jewelry. The old ladies in the coffins no longer needed it. Played against major chefs in Vegas. Learned cooking. Organized roving crap games that gathered after work on payday. They never knew what happened. Pulled together a team of associates to make money off the crooked insurance companies. Fooled the feds, kept a pile of money. Never had a traffic ticket. Raised a big family. Married three pretty women. Had two boys by young women that I didn't marry. Drove a Cadillac. Built finest houseboat on any lake, and good houses for me and the children—decorated and landscaped. Traveled first-

class. People knew me in Vegas. Dined on the very best. Owed no man. After the trucking period had no mortgages. Never broke for more than one day. Made money in prison. Self-made. Self-taught. Winnings and sales profits—cash a plenty. Five grand in my right front pocket. No bank-account. Paid in cash. Helped little children. Improved the family wealth of associates. Had lots of friends. Spread insurance company's money around. Whipped many a man without ever throwing a punch. Never killed anybody. Kept good guns, not on person. Backed winners in politics. Fooled the neighbors but treated them good. Had lots of lies told about me—dumped bodies in waterways, cheated at the table, investigated in wife's murder, mistreated a minor. Other than insurance fraud, nothing ever proven, never charged. Refused to gamble with locals. Imported players for home games. Left enough on the table for the loser to get home on. Loyal to the family. Always had a clean shirt.

Mornings usually present a clearer mind. It's a time for planning, for thankfulness for health, friends, food, necessities. Guilt or concerns of the previous day fade. Recently my morning thoughts continue the tract—what Grifton thought. I read some place that one can think of two words that have no known connection: thimble-cloud, for example; or paper-chair. Supposedly this relieves the obsessing. I might try it. But today, new fodder is needed.

GRIFTON GOES DEEP

A trumpet blast, the horses are off; a bugle sounds and the troops rise; a bell rings and lunch is served. I heard none of these as I dressed for the day. The doorbell did stay the buttoning of my last cuff. Few people call these days. Occasionally someone comes by, seeking a loan (never to be repaid) of twenty dollars or so. These callers never get out before midmorning or early afternoon. A doorbell ring unlike a knock reveals little. The knock may be frantic, gentle, embarrassed, hard, demanding. At seven a.m. I opened the door to a tall, fit, suited, salt and pepper grey, serious-looking man. "You, Grant, Caleb Grant?"
I said, "yes."
He said this in a clear, firm voice filled with authority. "My name is Bunch, Officer Claude Bunch from the FBI." Flinching at the passing of a patrol car, examining the odometer, touching my billfold for license, considering car's lighting, the glove-box for title. That very nearly describes me. Faced with a live FBI agent, I stepped back from the door, and stammered, "Come in, Mr. Bunch". A quick mental review turned up no federal infractions. One never knows for sure. My hand shook slightly as I gestured for him to follow into the living room. "How may I be of service, sir," I asked, while trying to control any nervousness in my voice.
"Mr. Grant, I'm working on a multi-state criminal case that you may have unknowingly interfaced with." I quickly assured him that I knew nothing about any multi-state criminals and certainly had no connection with such. Spend twenty years in lock-up, but innocent, convicted of a murder without knowing anything about it. These thoughts and others flicked through my mind.
"Mr. Grant, I'm not here to investigate you."
Trying to be nonchalant, I said, "good."
Bunch continued, "Are you acquainted with Crit Rose?"

"Not really," I said.

"You were observed visiting his house." Bunch gave me the date.

"Sorry, sir, I thought you meant was I acquainted with Mr. Rose. I did briefly visit his house, after meeting him in a diner. These encounters hardly allowed for an actual acquaintance."

"No matter, I'm here to warn you that your path merged with an extremely dangerous man. We've been on this case off and on for several years and just now have enough evidence to initiate a round-up." More relaxed now, I ask the particulars. Bunch said he wasn't privileged to give specifics, but did mention money laundering, guns, gambling, illegal transport of migrants across state lines. "Get the gist?" I did, but any connection to me evaded me. "We have tapes of your discussion with Crit and know of your Grifton Davis interest." With that Bunch sat far back on the couch, stretched his legs out and began. "Grifton Davis, like you, didn't know who he was associating with back in the day. We knew about their gambling sprees and companions. Davis was small time, his crimes local, nothing violent to our knowledge. However, he was sucked in during one of these gatherings by a Randolph Gregorvich from Detroit—not the best of a citizen, I might add."

Detroit, black silk shirt, I remembered him from Crit's discussion regarding the gaming table seating. He sat between Crit and Paducah, I think, during their gambling meets.

Bunch leaned further back crunching the couch, his hands behind his head, clasping his wrist as a fifteen a year-old tape began, nothing but static in the beginning. It was to reveal a remarkable tale. Bunch proceeded with this as though he had all the time necessary and was talking to someone who needed to know. Turns out, for me, the information was more interesting than helpful.

A win—on the court, or in a classroom spelling contest, a debate, or a boxing match, and especially at the gaming table—adds wind to the victor, power to his limbs, word usage to his vocabulary. This rush oftentimes dims reality, clouds judgement.

The tape and the story: Grifton had just taken the pot including the twenty-thousand deposits at a Crit Rose fall rendezvous. Bunch started and stopped the tape to add clarification. Randolph Gregorvich leaned in beside Grifton at the hors d' oeuvres' table. Crit had Bell County cornered discussing the coal related depression in Eastern Kentucky. Paducah was dancing with the remaining attendant who seemed reluctant to leave.

Randolph punched Grifton in the ribs with his forefinger as though to let excess wind out. "Youse guys like a bounce in your family wealth?" Grifton, rubbed wrong by the punch in the ribs, and feeling pert with winnings, leaned in close. "What do you mean youse guys? I'm my own man."

Randolph not wanting to lose his prospect said he meant "nuttin" and began his proposition. "I'm talking clams, lots of clams."

To this Grifton smiled, shook his head, and said, "What"?

"Money, Country Boy, big money." Grifton chafed a little over being called country by this apparently self-proclaimed city boy. Money! Was that so hard to say? "I might balk."

"Balk?" Randolph didn't understand.

"Yeah, Balk. Fall back against the singletree, rear against the tongue chain."

Randolph, having no idea what Grifton meant, plunged ahead, "A hundred thousand plus room, board, flight tickets, car rental, just south of Sarasota, Florida; work six weeks during January and February; run the table six nights a week, and win." Randolph raised his voice as he said, "WIN". Randolph had observed Grifton long enough to know that when Grifton dealt, he determined the winner.

High on himself, high on his full briefcase, Grifton agreed on the spot—not knowing how deep he was about to go, not asking who was involved, not thinking about his roving crap games, his loafing down at the Chevron Station, his planning the insurance scam, his pretty wife in their lovely home. The confidence generated by the night's win, the thought of a hundred thousand dollars guaranteed, and the warm Florida sun consumed his thoughts.

Florida was everything Grifton had hoped—warm sunshine, good food and plenty of it, dealing to and defeating a range of high-rollers from across the country. He was boarded in an apartment attached to an excellent restaurant where servings were huge. Even though he didn't have to pay, he noticed that prices were uncommonly low. In fact, dinner servings were so large, he boxed enough for apartment snacks. The establishment accepted only cash, no cards or checks. He decided that this might be a way they laundered a portion of the winnings from the tables. Any food audit would reveal quantities sufficient for a much larger clientele than the number served. No cost tickets were produced, merely slips listing the meal. Tracking the income was impossible since the slips were easily altered.

Grifton's apartment was on the second floor. Stairways inside and out led down to the first and ground levels. Neither stair accessed the third floor. But enter the first-floor apartment, then proceed through the kitchen in the rear to a small closet door hidden behind the huge commercial cook stove. Beyond the door a dank, dark stairway led to the basement. There behind the shelves of food, and the wine racks was an elevator lifting to the third floor, the only way up and down. At first this single access concerned Grifton about fire emergency, but the excitement of the game soon replaced any fear.

The third-floor gaming room accommodated seven dealers, plus three crap tables and the players. Beyond the playing area, couches and comfortable leather covered chairs were arranged for breaks. Double doors led to a full bar and dining room which served complete meals. A dorm sleeping room off to the right allowed for ancillary activities.

Randolph brought Grifton up to date on the play; four outside players and one house player to each table. The house player changed every three or so hours, rotating to the crap tables. A few visiting players won some. Others lost plenty. The house always won. The house profited. Grifton's quick hands dealt to the house player. Only once did anyone question the game. A tall slow-talking Texan said, "Seems your luck is powerfully good" to the house player. No further comments were made, and Grifton played on.

In mid-February, his time up, Grifton was directed to travel some miles inland to receive his pay. At the address, a small nineteen-fifties style ranch house sat back from the rural state road on what Grifton assumed was a large tract of land with fishing pond, riding stable, and tennis court. A gentle looking older fellow invited him in, offered coffee, and seated him in a small living room. The couch cover was worn thin, as was the carpet. The gentleman, wearing house shoes, sweats, and tee shirt retrieved a book from the coffee table in front of them. What at first appeared to be a page marker turned out to be a cashier's check drawn for the agreed upon one hundred thousand dollars.

Handing the check to Grifton, the elderly house resident said, "You did well, Davis." Grifton had declined the offer of coffee and was dismissed without getting the man's name. At the front door, Grifton was stopped. Clasping his arm in a grip that Grifton thought defied the gentleman's age, he said, "Davis, I'd invite you to join us, but there is too much blood on the tables for a man like you". The older man looked serious or sad, Grifton thought. Just as well, Grifton was homesick, homesick for the hills, homesick for his own operation where he better understood who and what he was looking for when he looked over his shoulder. Bunch stared hard at me suddenly. "I expect you're wondering why the Agency is going around showing an old tape and telling an old story." I was, but said nothing, just smiled and shrugged, sure that he was going to tell. The next part of his report made more sense. The case against Crit and company had been pretty-well developed years ago when orders came down from above, according to Bunch. His department was ordered to put everything on hold and focus all resources on terror. Bunch looked at me as if to say, you can understand that. He continued the report.

"The case lay dormant all these years until the national domestic gun violence exploded. We hadn't been looking at the Crit case. Crit and his associates came up in an investigation involving a drugs-for guns case, the trail running from Florida to Detroit to Chicago."

By the time the case was re-opened, Crit's father, the old paymaster encountered in Florida by Grifton, had passed and Crit was running the company, but not from Florida. Instead headquarters had moved to the Knobs here in Kentucky. Bunch drew a circle with his forefinger. "You see, Mr. Grant, we get our man, though it sometimes may take a circuitous route, we always get him." He presented a very smug, knowing smile and reached to shake hands. Having completed his report that sounded more like a novella than an FBI report, Bunch gathered his tape recorder (which played a very minor role in the report) and said his farewell. The morning story hadn't added much for my report, but it was interesting. I enjoyed Bunch much more than first expected.

The morning gone, I set about ordering the rest of my day. Something the visit had prevented me doing had to be next—reading the news briefs on my phone. This included Bloomberg, CBS, CNBC, CNN, Fox, Politico, WSJ, WP,

NBC, Popular Science; all required reading in my opinion, but each to be screened carefully for editorial bias. Funny, the first article I read covered the Trump-Bannon squabble over *Wolfe's, "Fire and Fury" book*. What if my report to the Davis men generated an explosive response similar to the President's toward Mr. Bannon's comments quoted in the book?

AMOS MOON NEEDS HELP

Mandy came in from the back deck after Bunch left, eager to find out who he was, and what we were talking about so long. "FBI," I said, for full effect.

"FBI, what in the world?" She blurted this out loud enough for the neighbors to hear. I patted her shoulder, sat her down and reported an abbreviated version of Bunch's story. "So," she said, "he was warning you to be careful." I explained that Crit Rose and I had absolutely no connection other than the inquiry I'd made about Grifton's gambling, that I was perfectly safe and so was our name, provided she didn't talk to anyone about the interview with Bunch. I hoped that she abided by this last admonition. Interesting secrets are often hard to keep, and good stories tend to grow.

Mandy returned to her back-deck project—adding a wax finish to a treasure she'd found at Goodwill—I   to the newspaper office. I had filed an article featuring a local hero who distinguished himself in WWII. Some of the report contained claims that the editor was questioning. If he traveled the Pacific islands, carrying a gun, facing the enemy, and got back in one piece, he was a hero to me. If he captured more machine gun nests, more enemy combatants than seemed humanly possible, good for him. If memory enhanced his importance in the cause, who was I to question. The editor finally agreed, and I left.

Instead of going directly to my car, I crossed the street to the Family Diner. Having missed lunch due to the Bunch interview, reviewing it with Mandy, and then the news editor meeting, I was hungry; a grilled cheese sandwich and coffee, perhaps. Just inside the door W. H. Harrison commanded the first table enjoying his early afternoon coffee break. I was invited to join him and took a chair across from W. H and next to Amos Moon who was not looking right. His eyes were dull, his shirttail was askew, one shoe was untied. He could easily have passed for someone in a jail interview room, brought in for drunken driving. He wasn't drunk, however. As usual W. H. had charge of the discussion, continuing his discourse.

"Go ahead, Amos, you're among friends. Friends have assisted friends over rough spots since mankind began talking to one another. I'm guessing that's what the *Canterbury Tales* were about when you get down to it." I'd never thought about the Tales in that light, but W. H. often talked in hyperbole when relaxing his cafe-table audience.

"W. H., I'm thinking this is serious." Amos went on to tell about a row he and his wife were involved in. He pointed out to his wife a few days ago that President Trump's new tax law was going to benefit everybody. She stormed out of the house and went to her mother's, that is, after two days of this back and forth, devolving into a rage. Everything from the wall between the U.S. and Mexico, the president's lying, philandering, being super rich, tampering with the EPA, denying global warming were brought up. The worst though, according to Amos, was her hanging up on him each time he called at her mother's. She had now been gone three nights, the most she'd ever stayed away. Amos was sure the marriage was over. He was starving, and the cat hadn't been home for two of the three nights. Amos was dabbing his dull eyes by this time, his head slumping more with each revelation.

"Amos, listen. What I'm about to reveal to you are certain facts, and Caleb here will back me up, that all men must learn." W. H. had scooted back in his chair and was looking over Amos's head, I suspected trying to think what to say next. "Take Lady Macbeth, said to be a composite of two historical figures that the great Shakespeare created. She portrays womanhood to a tee. Oh, I don't mean all women are heartless, I merely use this analogy to demonstrate. The Lady wanted a man killed, then she was destroyed by guilt over the act. Women, Amos, aren't as physically strong as men. Skills to get around this weakness, you see, are likely evolutionarily acquired.

"Say you make the missus mad. She can't get you down on the floor and thrash you for it, so she throws a tantrum while you stand with your palms up hoping she recognizes this passivity as an apology; she stays away from your bed three nights, leaving you to shiver and wonder. Punishment, you see.

"In your case something else is in the mix. She, along with most women in the country, see Trump's behavior toward their sisters as abhorrent, unforgivable. This becomes an overlay, so to speak, nothing positive about the man is ever acknowledged. Anything you or I, or Caleb says of a positive nature about the man is an attack on the sisterhood.

"Lucky for you and all mankind, for that matter, women have another side—the mother instinct. Notice how the most needful men keep their wives subservient. These men need a mother. The wife naturally falls into the pattern of fetching, waiting on, rubbing sore muscles for these fellows. Now you take men like us, rugged individualists, a woman is not likely to rub our sore muscles." W. H. chuckled and pulled his shirt cuff down below his suit coat.

"Reckon she'll come home, W. H.?" Amos was looking more pitiful than ever.

"Of course, she'll come home. Won't she, Caleb?" I looked hard at W. H., not frowning or smiling for Amos's benefit, but certainly the answer to W. H.'s question was not in my head. I gave the slightest nod. W. H. picked up again.

"Amos, once the Missus hears about you being down here at the diner, looking all disheveled, talking to your attorney, maybe about a will, and not eating a bite, that mother instinct will kick in. She'll be back. Now the best thing you can do is go home. Walk up and down in front of your house several times a day, don't change clothes or clean up in any way. Let the neighbors see the distress you're experiencing. Rest assured she'll hear. Her resistance will give way to pity. She'll remember how good you are at taking out the trash, how she enjoys seeing you eat her cornbread. Cornbread reminds me, somebody is sure to report a certain divorcee or widow lady knocking at your backdoor carrying a dishcloth covered pan."

"But nobody has brought food." Amos shook head as he reported this.

W. H. looked at me and winked. "No matter, some busybody will give such a report. Sometimes it works wonders too."

Still looking sad and pitiful, and now confused, Amos thanked W. H. profusely, asked that we say nothing to Knot Head about the discussion and made his way out. As Amos passed outside our window, I saw the fear, confusion in his eyes, the slump of his shoulders. Men like Amos reach old age not knowing certain parameters that encircle love. Oftentimes the love lines touch or almost touch the anger line, coming from the other way, a line that borders on hate. When the two lines get close or meet, little reasoning abounds. Men strike out, women leave. The anger-hate line needs time to cool when these thresholds cross. No one ever masters the line that prevents overheating. Most people gradually learn to recognize the flashpoints and avert the blowout using certain words, practicing evasive actions, or extending a gentle touch. Other marriages cannot tolerate such heat and break-up.

W. H. drained his coffee cup, leaned in close to me and asked if the Grifton report was finished. I told him no, but that it was coming together. "Hellfire, Caleb, you'd better take my advice and two-sentence that report. That's not only my opinion, that's my legal opinion." With that he crammed his hat on his head, said good day and tromped out.

Mandy yelled from somewhere toward the back bedroom as I entered the house—somewhat frantic, I thought. Laying my note binder and hat aside, I made my way back through the house as quickly as possible, noticing an empty soup bowl, a water glass and silverware on the dining table as I passed. Once in the bedroom I caught, *the look*. That look that all men recognize. Then I saw the table wedged between the bed and the far wall. Mandy had finished putting the wax on her table while I was out. She deemed it a night stand to sit between the bed and the far wall. The round stand that the table sat on was down between the wall and bed, but the top, too large to fit, hung on the edge of the huge bed, and lodged against the wall on the far side. Mandy, wedged against the wall with the bed and the table blocking any movement could go neither way. "I fixed soup for your lunch," she said dourly.

The bed, big enough to sleep an entire family, not only takes a half-day to change the sheets, it is extremely heavy—too heavy for Mandy and me to lift and shift, even if she were in a proper position. After viewing the situation, I told Mandy I'd have to get off to myself and study about the problem a few minutes. Again, I got *the look*. Nevertheless, I went to the kitchen, poured myself a glass of water and pondered. The sons-in-laws were at work for another two hours. The only close neighbors were too infirm to help. Finally, I settled on something that always worked on the farm and went to the barn for the spud bar (a long steel rod flat on one end used to break ice when ice fishing, a rock in the bottom of a posthole, or as a lever to move heavy logs in the log woods). With a long enough lever, a man can lift and shift the earth, I had heard said back in high school physical science. I freed Mandy and set the night stand but had to heat my own soup for supper.

ACE AND DUCE TELL THEIR TALES

Mandy was in a much better mood the next morning. She and her sis had made plans to visit the Goodwill Store. A certain item was passing the thirty-day limit—this information whispered to Mandy by the volunteer clerk who is also in Mandy's DAR. Prices are dropped fifty per cent on the thirty-first day of display. Mandy and Eunice had selected a must-have lamp that was to be marked down. They were leaving early, determined to close the deal. I completed my Toasted Oats in milk, topped with fruit, and began the ritual of reading the news on the phone when a call came through from Ace.

"Mr. Grant, this is Ace Davis." Ace went on to explain his mission. "I's wondering if you'd mind me and Duce looking at Pap's old boat. We didn't get to spend much time on it as boys, but we remember it being a good outfit." I said, "no, of course, you are welcome to tour it anytime". I had no intention, however, of letting them visit the boat without my being on board. Neither did I appreciate him referring to it as Pap's old boat, it being as pristine as the day of the transfer. We agreed to meet at the boat later in the morning. He explained that Duce was still asleep.

I arrived ahead of the Davises, donned my deck shoes, and prepared a jug of lemonade. Ace and Duce came aboard, Duce stepping high and talking fast—his fix apparently at work. From stem to stern and back they moved, stopping to examine and discuss. Duce pointed out where he was when he fell overboard in the middle of Lake Cumberland. "Pap had to come in after me." He laughed at this.

"What I remember is that time you yanked the throttle to full speed and threw Pop down on the deck. You 'bout got one over that." Ace hit Duce on the shoulder as he made this comment. Both went down on the deck, Duce tripping Ace and falling on top. They came up laughing. I relaxed, thinking the alpha male merely swapping back and forth between intellect and brute strength. Below deck Duce opened the refrigerator, peered in and slammed it shut. The two climbed on the master bed, tried the headsets and tuned the televisions to *The Andy Griffith Show,* smiling at one another obviously experiencing a childhood memory. The looking, touching, trying lasted the better part of an hour. I finally invited them to join me on deck for lemonade.

Once settled at the table Ace and Duce began alternating, each telling his funny story—all contained an unhealthy pathology. Duce paced back and forth after presenting his first adventure, but always within hearing and commenting. Finally, Ace drained his lemonade, lit a cigarette, leaned back far in his chair, and crossed his legs at the ankle. Looking at Duce, he said, "Remember that time we hijacked the Walmart truck."

"Hijacked it hell! It hijacked me best I remember."

Ace smiled, puffed and ask, "How old were we?"

"Seventeen or eighteen, I guess."

"No. No. We didn't have license to drive. I think we might have been fifteen. We were still in Illinois. Uncle had an old flatbed truck he used for odd jobs and let us drive it on the backroads. One of the backroads ran close to the regional Walmart warehouse, just a field separating it from our route. Duce got the idea to rob one of their trucks."

"There must have been hundreds of them coming and going, all filled with good stuff, and more profitable than shoplifting. That was my thinking." Duce had stopped pacing and was looking out across the lake.

"I dropped Duce off at the truck entrance." Ace was smiling as he flipped his cigarette butt over the railing.

"I got inside the gate, ran like hell till I found an open trailer, loaded too. First thing I realized was that everything was packed on pallets and tied tight as a banger string with tough metal straps. No way could I manage a pallet or remove a strap. Looking over the pallets I could see a box or two stored on top, unstrapped. I plundered my way over and around the shitin' things. Each unstrapped box that might have been pilfered contained tooth paste or some such. Just as I reached the front of the trailer, CLANK I heard the door slam—closest thing I've heard was a jail door." Duce looked at me for a response. I made none.

"The place was dark as pitch. I lurched and pitched, seemed like a damned month before the truck stopped, till I got to see daylight."

Since they both survived, I laughed with them. Ace took over. "I followed that truck till nearly dark before it backed into a loading dock behind a super Walmart. Thought sure as frigging shit I'd run out of gas before it stopped. The driver went inside with his hand-held inventory monitor. He must have been off schedule or ate dinner or something. He was gone forever. Next thing I knew a security guard had my forearm in a tight squeeze jerking me awake and out of the truck."

Ace scratched under his arm and continued his narrative. "Security guards held us out behind the truck. The big dude called the local police. Deciding what to charge us with was harder than you think." Ace was gnawing at his thumbnail.

Duce was charged for trespassing, and Ace for driving without a license. Things had gotten more complicated though when the uncle was called in to arrange for their release. He was to pay the driving violation fine and truck tow. Duce was to appear in court. Instead of paying and getting them released, the uncle declared that they were out of control.

"'They can't read or write, won't work, and they run the roads at all hours of the night.' That's what our uncle told the judge." A female cousin had convinced the uncle that placement in a facility for the developmentally handicapped might bring the boys around—*New Hope,* it was called. The cousin's boy-friend had once worked there.

Duce spoke up. "Unk had us sent to the 'sylum, the old shithead."

Ace mumbled as he licked his thumbnail. "Wasn't that bad, didn't last long. We got our heads together while they were trying to figure out what was wrong with us. They gave us crazy tests. Look at this, what do you see kind of thing, ask a million questions, tried to do a Kentucky background check, which they couldn't. They gave us puzzles to work. It went on all day. We decided if crazy is what you want, crazy is what you get." Ace got up and walked around on the deck. I decided we probably could all use a break and took the men down to the galley for chicken soup and crackers.

After the two wolfed down the soup, a half-box of crackers, and drank another jug of lemonade, Ace, eager to tell all, began. "They put us in a house with close neighbors. The fellow supervising the six of us didn't act just right, I thought. Our roommate stumbled around, talked to himself, and hung on to the social worker every time she got close. One of the others slipped out and ran through the neighborhood at least once a day. What me and Duce did was work our plan."

"Our plan, hell! Your plan. I was to draw my own blood!" Duce rubbed his forearm as he said this.

Ace grinned. "The plan was for me to set fires around the house; not dangerous fires, just toilet tissue, clean-ex tissue, things like that. Burnt it close to the wall so as to smoke the paint a little. Duce's job was to steal a knife from the kitchen and cut his initials on door facings and about."

"Yeah, tell him what else I had to do."

"Well, Duce was to draw blood from his forearm and leave bloody toilet paper around."

"Caleb, you can see from that who the daddy of the plan was. He didn't have to draw any blood with a dull kitchen knife." Duce had a serious frown, his brows knit. The memory was not good.

Ace lowered his voice for the finale. "We got committed on Saturday morning and released to Unk on Wednesday the following week. The supervisor declared us unsuited for the placement—a danger to the other residents, out of control. Incorrigible, or something like that, was stamped on the folder given to Unk." Ace was slapping the table and laughing, Duce was leaning back over the countertop howling. I laughed a little.

The men left after completing their tale, convinced that they had provided entertainment sufficient for the day. After cleaning up the galley, I went topside and sat, enjoying the lake breeze, replaying the Davis brothers' story, comparing it with previously gathered information. The uncle's statement about them not being able to read at fifteen was baffling. Certainly, their verbal skills were adequate. Admission to an adolescent facility for the developmentally disabled generally indicates an IQ of around sixty. That doesn't appear to apply in their case. It is possible they have a reading disorder or have experienced inadequate educational experiences. Everything is speculative, but this referral and admission sounds a little fishy. The uncle and the cousin were merely working the system, maybe to deceive the courts or the state's social services personnel. That was my conclusion anyway.

The day had been interesting, fun actually. But the lesson was clear: intervention with the two Davis men—not likely. Later, Mandy and I were home in the den watching *Jeopardy* and enjoying coffee and a sugar free brownie. During a commercial break I, for the umpteenth time, stated my frustration with the Grifton project. We had already discussed the Ace and Duce tale over dinner. "Why don't you go back to Forrest, your original source?" Mandy turned her attention to the next program question, leaving me to study. My answer turned out to be: why not. She is so handy to have around.

FORREST HAS ANOTHER PEACHY CONNECTION

I walked over to Forrest's house all the time doubting finding him at home. There he was though sitting out under a huge maple tree beside the house, a large tub directly in front of him, an apple in one hand, a paring knife in the other. Paper thin skins were piled at his feet. I said, "Hi'dy".

Forrest smiled his usual congenial smile and said, "Come over, Caleb. I'm needing a break. My fingers are numb." He dropped his knife among the apple slices. Sheared cores lay among the peels. He wiped his hands on a towel that spread across his legs. I saw, as I got closer, that the tub was nearly half-full of red, fall apples. For an instant, I saw and tasted Mandy's smooth sweet jelly spread on a hot buttered biscuit.

In the huge tub, the unpeeled apples were floating in clear water, a green leaf, a stem here and there. To Forrest's left sat three or four full pans—white fruit peeled and neatly sliced. Seeing me eying the pans, Forrest moved his head in a short nod. "The woman's freezing them."

We moved to lounge chairs on the other side of the great maple, but still in the shade with a better view of the lake where fishermen sat high in bass boats jiggling their tackle. After considerable small talk, some gossip, and need to know community news, I repeated the tales Ace and Duce had shared with me on the boat.

"I don't recollect nothing about that" was all Forrest said as he bent and rubbed his ankle. "Durn yellow jacket stung me a few minutes afore you come." Seeing a brown lump l asked if it was still hurting. "No," he said. "I put a chew of 'baccer on it. Draws the pain and swelling right out." He extended his chin and said, "a lot of people don't know that." I agreed.

Forest suddenly bumped his forehead with his palm as people sometimes do when remembering something.

"Caleb, I've run into something. Been meaning to call you."

Thinking he was probably referring to my Grifton interest, I leaned toward him. "What?"

"Well, you know Peachy died."

I shook my head, frowned and said, "Yes."

"Well, her landlady was cleaning out her room, had some stuff in it she didn't know what to do with. Her name is Elnora Begley, one of the Begley's from over on Buck Creek. Good people." Forrest's eyes opened wide for emphasis at this last remark. His serious face now pointed toward me. "She remembered Peachy's brother Del but didn't know where to find him. After calling around, my name come up and she called me, said she had some of Peachy's things, could she bring them over. I said okay, and she dropped off a bag full of clothes and a jewelry box. Wife give the clothes to Goodwill. The box had a lot of bangles in it. You won't believe what else." I raised my eyebrows as if to say go on.

"They was some writing. That weren't all neither. I found a diamond ring worth a right smart, I reckon." I remembered the diamonds the dancing lady left Grifton and he gave one to Peachy, which Del thought to be lost. My interest lay with the writing. I asked Forrest about the writing. "There's three or four pages folded in the bottom of the box, look like letters she wrote." He nodded vigorously.

As I was leaving, Forrest gave me the writing. "You can have these," he said. I declined.

"I'll return them later. Some of the family likely will be interested in these in years to come; someone trying to fit the pieces of who they are, where they came from," I said. "Um-hum," Forrest said, as he hugged me. "God Bless You".

I stepped lively going home, eager to read Peachy's writing, the closest thing to direct communication I hoped to get. Four documents, possibly letters, maybe never shared with anyone, were in the box. Forrest had removed the bangles and the diamond. I'll have to admit to having an uncertain, uncomfortable feeling as I removed the first page—guilt likely. To me, reading a girl's diary was beyond the pale, right out there with voyeurism, but this wasn't exactly a diary.

Page one began: "Mom," written in beautiful script at the top; no address, date, nothing else to identify its origin.

Mom

I remember when Del and I were little, he dressed in little blue, dressy shorts with suspenders, a white short sleeved shirt, saddle oxfords, and hat (like the Hipsters wear); I in a pink dress with daisies around the waist, trimmed at the neck with lace, and black patent leather shoes, a straw hat with a pink ribbon hanging over the brim in back. You took us to church, the big church building on the corner, with huge columns out front. Older people greeted you, asked your name and hugged Del and me. I didn't want to get mussed. The hugs weren't that pleasant. Del seemed pleased with the attention. That's the only time I remember us going to church. After the service, about all I could remember was the description of Hell. The thought haunted me for some time. It still does, in fact. At that time, I was in second, third or fourth grade, I am not sure. Del wasn't in school.

You and I often sat at the kitchen table at night. Sometimes I sat on your lap, smelled your perfume, felt your body against mine, and read to you. You applauded when I pronounced a seemingly hard word. Later, when Del and I went to bed, you read a chapter book to us. Del was usually sound asleep before the chapter was finished. I can feel your lips now on my forehead as you kissed me good night. Those memories fade as I think of the middle school years. Where did you go? The three of us were still together. You were cooking, cleaning, delivering us from place to place, yet it seems that Del and I were forgotten, on our own, left to figure out life for ourselves. Later we were with Grifton, things were happening in the house that children should not have seen. I've learned that Moms should be like the old mother lion, guarding her cubs at all times, at any expense. You were not a lioness. We solved our own problems as inexperienced children, often falling into paths better avoided. Beyond the early childhood years, you dropped us—rearing completed. Well, I wish I could tell you rearing wasn't completed. I had questions that needed answers, woman answers. Who was I to turn to? Grifton? Del? Not likely. Mostly I just figured out life, love, the future for myself. Sometimes I feel like only part of a person...

The note ended. Whether her mom ever saw it, whether it was written before her mother left Grifton and was killed, whether it was a complete document, whether it was written after dropping out of high school, whether she was on drugs at the time, there was no way of knowing. Interrupting Mandy's reading, I briefly described the note and convinced her to read it for second-eyes input. Mandy frowned rather seriously, I thought, before agreeing. She was deep in Ferber's book, *So Big*.

The second writing was laid-out the same as the first. It began, "Dad."

Dad:

I don't even know why I'm writing this. I never knew you, never saw you. Zero, that's what I get when trying to picture you, how you walked, talked, smelled—zilch. If mom had photos, memories, or even knew who you were, she never shared them. So, I know nothing of grandparents, or cousins on your side of the family, or even if Del is your son. My mind is void as to you. I'm pretty much just a half a person. I can't talk to you, can't even talk about you with any confidence. So why am I trying to write this. You don't exist. Only your DNA is present and how can that be questioned, except to ask if therein lies whatever makes me like I am...

The third note was set up the same as the first two, except it had Grifton at the top.

Grifton

You were there and you weren't there. You helped and you hurt. You were never Dad, just Grifton the slippery, Grifton the absent, Grifton the builder, Grifton the provider, Grifton the showman, Grifton from the dark, dirty hollow, always scratching, shoveling trying to fill that lonesome, isolated spot from your past.

One time you took us to Florida, you going to gamble most likely. Anyway, it was exciting for Del and me. He gathered shark's teeth, sand dollars, and watched for dolphins. I did cart wheels on the beach, wore Mom's sunglasses and tried to look cool. You came in from the beach the very first day in swim trunks and flipflops. Stopping before the long mirror in the living room of our condo, you said, "The eighty-year old girls down on the beach do not resemble mermaids." You looked at mom and laughed. Then said, "I look more like a manatee, you think?" You then sucked in your tummy and headed to the bathroom. That was funny and it wasn't funny. That's the way you were.

Mom later told me that you bragged about walking the beach asking the old ladies if they were happily married, that is, those with larger diamonds on their fingers and holding no man's arm. Mom said you were fishing for one who was game enough to join the late-night table. I bet that was true. What else were you to do? You had no work there or source of income so far as I knew, and you were gone day and night on several occasions.

There was one morning, actually it was probably afternoon, I heard Mom crying in the bedroom. You had been gone three days and was sleeping in. I leaned hard against the bedroom door and heard you say, "Don't worry, I'm working a plan. I'll get it back."

I thought we were broke and told Del. For the next two days we worried about how we'd get home. Then you came in carrying your briefcase, opened it on the kitchen table and asked Del and me to count the contents. We did the best we could. Finally, you winked at Mom and said, "Oh, I'll tell you how much is in it." Del and I relaxed after that. Looking back, I'm guessing you had set somebody up for a big surprise. That's what I was hearing through the door. Mom must have thought you were broke too.

An ugly, grotesque actually, picture passed through my mind for years; you and the elderly woman dancing around in the house, everybody clapping, yelling, sloshing drinks, her dress up around her hips, her trying to undress. Thinking that was an okay scene for an early adolescent to experience is beyond me. I may have been thirteen. Figuring out womanhood on my own was hard enough without the examples common in our household. I say our household. Actually, it never felt like ours. It was yours. We occupied it for a time. You were always talking about building Mom's dream home, especially after she left. It was your dream home. We all knew that. "Take off your shoes inside. Don't use the jacuzzi, I'm nailing your window shut." We got the message.

Then there was the stepbrother. I was deathly afraid of him, nothing that I could specifically identify, but somehow, intuitively, I knew he was dangerous. Sure enough, he proved it when he was sent to prison. In a way our home was a beautiful house of horrors. A home cannot be judged from the other side of closed doors. Don't misunderstand, I don't blame you for everything that's happened in my life. I've had choices...

Again, the note seemed incomplete. I decide to sleep on these findings and take up the task the next morning while fresh. When I got to bed, Mandy moved over and granted me one of the pillows. "I'm in no shape to discuss it." That was all she said. I got the message. The note she'd read was disturbing. Mothers see things others miss. They cleanse their minds of disturbing input differently.

The following morning was even more disappointing. Peachy almost reached out to someone. Almost. The note headed, Ms. Alma, was meant for the high school teacher, Mandy's and my friend who had invested so much in Peachy's development, who had tried so hard to locate her when she disappeared from school, to draw her back—to reap the benefits of her obvious potential.

Ms. Alma

I knew you were trying to reach me after I left school. I couldn't. I just couldn't...

The writing stopped abruptly. There is no question, this was unfinished. Embarrassment, shame, emotional turmoil or all three may have been at work. It's the saddest of the four notes for me, knowing what I do about Alma's concern, her special efforts. A good teacher has such an impact on youngsters. So pleasant it is to hear of teacher intervention and subsequent smooth sailing for a child after a period of internal turmoil. Alma's guilt, ill founded, but nonetheless real and lasting all these years makes me hurt for her even today.

(No Heading)

Scribbled on the back of Alma's note, apparently to no one in particular: *"I am miserable when high and more miserable when I'm sober; would it have been better to have gotten married; to have children, and to stay with the children to the end; to finish high school, to go to college? I just couldn't take my baggage in on somebody, to marry, to alter their life to who knows what end. The end for me? Motherhood copied from home life? I don't think so. Likely my end will come in a daze. Mom, a minus, Grifton, no better. Where was my pattern? Poor Del and me— dependent on me. What did I know?"*

The scribbling barely legible, not written in the neat script the other notes were in, written in time of anguish, anguish because of where she was in life, who she had become, who she had been destined to become from the beginning. I could be wrong, but I'm thinking environment, environment, environment—generations of environment. Blame is often placed on neighborhood, poverty, unemployment, ignorance. None of these fit for Peachy. Mental issues maybe, but I'm inclined to think the insecurity, the on-going attempt to ease pain, coupled to whatever happened behind the closed doors of that house, and whatever didn't happen there determined the outcome in Peachy's life.

Family is a complex institution. It's a simple institution. It works or doesn't work depending mostly on one principle—love. Love is both the complex and the simple. It's both inherent and learned. It may not be possible to define love, but it's always recognizable—I likely read that someplace.

These thoughts are consuming me. I've got to back away. Get back on tract, listen for Grifton. Finish this task.

THE RESTART

Several months passed. I dropped the Grifton inquiry, having decided I was too immersed, wasting time that could be more profitably used. Family, church work, community needs, maintenance issues around the place took precedence. Mandy and I hadn't been on the boat in months.

I awoke this morning with a new lease, stain the barn, weed the garden patch, pursue Grifton all were competing for my new-found energy. The Grifton search won out. But where to turn next? I was motivated but not inspired.

Also, there was something inside: my mind not quite relaxed, thoughts were not flowing, lacking creative spark. Mandy made my decision, sending me on an errand to the corner pharmacy. On the way to the drug store I encountered W. H. ambling along the sidewalk, his head down, hat somewhat askew, cigar smoke rising and flowing behind him. "Hello W. H.," I said.

"Why, Caleb Grant, I had begun to think that, like *Candide,* you'd left the country, searching for the Golden Fleece or some such." W. H. chuckled and slapped me on the shoulder.

"Just a bit of a shutdown," I said, then added, "went home to tend my garden". His eyes twinkled. "And what about you?"

"Oh, I've been on a most important case, Caleb, took me across this great continent."

"Really?" I said. W. H. tugged at his hat against a gust of wind.

"Yes, Caleb, a very important trip to San Francisco, in fact, interesting place, not that I'd want to live there, understand—people in too big a hurry. Life is too short for that in my estimation." I nodded as though I fully understood. "All young people, Caleb, many of whom have already made their fortune, out of nothing, I might add. Oh, it's something, I guess, out there in the cloud, whatever that means."

He shook a leaf off his shoe. "I was down in the Frisco financial district, everybody rushing, hardly time to look at you. That's not the worst though; hellfire, they walked too fast. I couldn't keep up.

Strangest thing though, Caleb," W. H. looked intently at me, a special gleam in his eye. "Out in the residential district, everybody was leading from one to nine dogs." W. H. chuckled. "That's right, I saw a little ninety-pound lady leading nine dogs. These dog people each carried a plastic bag, full of dog shit. Hellfire around here dogs leave their droppings, another dog comes along and eats it. Now that's nature's way." He shook his big head, frowned, and looked at the clock on the court house down the block.

"I'm going to have to ambulate, Caleb, important business over at the courthouse. When you going to come visit, have a good talk? History, science, religion, politics all need a good review."

Pleased, I said, "Anytime."

"Tell you what, the wife is in Gatlinburg, Tennessee for a couple of days, some big church gathering, I think. Why don't you come by the house tonight? I'd love to talk now, but a big day confronts me. As I said, very important business down at the court, you understand." I said yes and agreed to a seven-p.m. rendezvous.

After leaving W. H., to get along to his important business, I stopped in at the corner grocery. It was quiet. The owner was at the register and hi'dy talk evolved to Grifton, as so many of my conversations do. Hoppy Goodin, the proprietor, is also a bi-vocational minister.

"You probably know, Caleb, I baptized Grifton just before his death. Wonderful experience." Hoppy went on to say that a phone call, the voice just a whisper, begged him to come soon as possible. After several repeats, he caught on to who was calling and why. The confession transpired in

Grifton's kitchen, and the baptism in a pan on the kitchen table. "Now, ain't that something?" Hoppy looked intently at me until I responded, yes, it was. Hoppy moved on to ring up my purchase and I said good day. He said, "have a blessed day."

I arrived at W. H.'s at the appointed time. He lunged right in as though we'd been together for hours. "Caleb, the psyche is an intriguing jumble, yet oftentimes predictable. Take Homer, for example, that poet of old. He knew that the Helen-Paris episode was a prelude to war, thus the great *Trojan war* epic revealed in poetry; never to have happened, at least according to earlier thinking, which I support, without Homer's foreknowledge; the blood, the gore, the peeling back of man, so to speak, by predicting the reaction of Menelaus and his cohorts, Homer got his story. Cross that barrier, Caleb, stealing a man's woman, trouble follows, you see—predictability from among the storehouse in the human brain."

When I first arrived at W. H.'s house, I had wanted to mention my troubled spirit. So, when W. H. stopped for breath, I did. He immediately switched topics and began his usual, and mostly unnecessary elucidation. "Caleb, I'm no analyst, don't pretend to be, just a common lawyer, sometimes referred to as counselor." He bit off the end a cigar, lit it, then, apparently on second thought, offered me one. I don't smoke, but what the heck, I accepted the nasty tasting thing and lit up too.

Smoke rose about W. H,'s head to settle and linger for years on the curtains, the ceiling, the walls for all to smell, and some to gag. Smokers are oblivious. I pretend to be. "The law, Caleb, is mostly about words, interpreting words, adding punctuation for clarity. Words are the easy part of law." W. H. is now taking an entirely different approach from our earlier discussion when he delved into Cicero. "The hard part, the art I like to say, is the counseling. The attorney must understand the psyche. Let me clarify a little." He harrumphed from deep in his throat and in his mellow bass voice began.

"Your troubled spirit now, for example." W. H. paused assuring my attention. "You have been convinced it came from the intense, compulsive some would say, interest in Grifton Davis. Let me present, if I may, an alternate scenario." Knowing he was going to anyway, I nodded. "Caleb, you are a little older than me, but don't forget I have heard the hawk holler a few times myself." We both smiled. "Ever think about your retirement, how good that last day on the job felt? No more schedules, paperwork, phone calls, irate visitors." W. H. took a deep puff and let the smoke out slowly as he examined the ash on his cigar. "Not long after, remember how nobody called? Nobody needed your wisdom. Few people showed interest as you discussed the important events of your previous life?"

I squirmed, adjusted my trouser crotch. "Oh. And have you noticed how long it takes you to make water?" We both shook our heads, making a moue. "What about bothering the wife at night?"

I'd had enough! "Where is this going W. H.?"

"I'll tell you exactly where it's going. We're getting old. Our bodies rebel. Our mind rebels. What we think is bothering us is not it at all. Subconsciously we are saying, no. I don't want to get old. Hellfire Caleb, everybody experiences this. Just recognize it and get on with life. And one other thing, give the Davis men a two-sentence report, as I have continued to recommend. Then forget Grifton Davis. Go to the garden. Groom your horse. Drink coffee with the boys." As our cigars became mere stubs, we said our good nights.

Walking to the car I was thinking. How much gardening can I do knowing the deer and raccoons will get the harvest? It doesn't take long to groom a horse. Conversation with the boys at McDonalds, a little now and then maybe. I got the message, however. The crib baby knows only the now, just as I know only today, this instant. Life is an uncertainty, each minute a treasure, complete with its mystery as to the next. Hope is so wondrously laid out for us in scriptures. Uncertainty, mystery, hope, all bound up in each minute granted us. I made a quick decision to focus on these. No more aging for me.

The Wall Street Journal recently published an article, *Why Our Mental Health Takes a Village:* "One person can't help us with every mood, not everyone is adept at handling every emotion," according to the article. I'm planning to evaluate the W. H. discussion, mostly his discussion. It didn't leave me feeling exactly relieved. His usual calming effect had not taken hold. Mandy might round out my village.

"I was talking to W. H. today." I wanted to get Mandy's take on the issue before it slipped my mind.

"Um-hmm." Mandy was engrossed with something on Facebook as we sat on the screened-in porch enjoying coffee and listening to the rain.

"He says I'm worried about getting old."

"What?" At least one of the words must have sparked an interest.

"Getting old," I said.

"What brought that up?"

I proceeded to tell her about the W. H. discussion. She laid aside her phone, pulled her housecoat closer, and gave me that examining look. "Everybody gets old or dies early," she finally said—barked actually. That was a big help. I took a long sip of coffee and looked down at the horse, standing near the barn gate. He's nine years old this spring, I thought. Wonder if he is enjoying mid-life or lamenting losing his youth? He may not even know how old he is.

"Caleb, you are one of the best adjusted older men I know. Most men your age stagger around and sleep between doctor visits, discuss their meds for all to hear."

I am blessed. Don't take much medicine. I do stagger though. Actually, I liked what she had said.

"You can't pay any attention to W. H. He thinks he knows everything, presents an in-depth contribution to any and all discussions, a bit of a bore, if you ask me." Mandy crossed her legs, opened her phone, punched in crosswords and settled back. "What's a four-letter word for, to ask a question?"

"Quiz," I said.

"See, you aren't doing so bad." She punched on her phone. Then, thinking of something else, she looked up. "You do say things to people, not considering the impact." She had my attention, and as usual when that happens, wasn't going to let go without a little reminding or teaching or something.

I interrupted her. "Ideas rush into my mind that need to be said. Besides, I forget them if I don't get them out quickly." She snickered. "That's part of what I mean. You don't screen your words. Sometimes you think you are joking, maybe you are, but enough truth is in what you often say that it hurts people. That's just an example of what I'm talking about. Another thing, you go around touting Trump's policies."

"Wait just a minute. My world view was set years ago. My support of these issues goes all the way back to Lincoln." Mandy's face reddened, her voice rose, she spread her fingers wide, waving her hands.

"Lincoln, my foot. No way he'd recognize these sell-out, fund-raising, guile mouths who go around claiming to be Republicans." This discussion was going down-hill fast, I decided. So much for Mandy's massaging a roiling psyche. Hoping to redirect, I said, "Remember that time when were first married? Your dad advised me to look 'high and wide' mornings when I came out of the house. What do you think he was actually meaning?"

"Just what he said. Be aware of your environment." Mandy looked back at her phone. I didn't know but what her dad was referring to the eye exercise practiced by the WWII pilots. No matter, I decided it was time to go to the barn before it gets too dark, check the tiler, groom the horse, might even go down to the McDonalds tomorrow.

GRIFTON'S REDEMPTION

"People make light of sickbed, deathbed, foxhole confessions, Caleb." I'd made what I now thought was a mistake—raising the issue of Grifton Davis's confession and baptism with William Harrison. We were sitting under a huge pin oak tree in front of the courthouse. The crowd had gone home for the day, and W. H. slid in beside me on the bench. I was just loafing and thinking. He was leaving court for the day.

W. H. had just gotten started. "Scripture addresses this issue several times, to my way of thinking."

I told him that I'd even heard preachers talk about doubting salvation under such duress.

"Oh, you have to look beyond the preachers, Caleb. The Creator has revealed himself to all men. All men in turn have tried to see, to appease, to arrive in his presence. Take the indigenous people of the Americas. They were looking to the great Spirit when the religious European arrived here. The early Egyptians, Greeks, Romans, I hold that all peoples had the same revelation."

I admitted that scriptures tell us that God revealed himself to all mankind, but most added their human interpretations, generally perverting the revelation—sacrificing babies, self-mutilation and so forth. "We're straying from the central subject here," I said.

"Not really. All I'm saying is that all mankind has a chance at salvation. If we accept that God is love, all-knowing, and all-powerful as opposed to a souped-up man out there someplace, a different picture emerges." I had no idea where W. H. was going with this. "Caleb, those men who doubt Grifton Davis's salvation have not read the entire scriptures. They're reacting out of pride, bringing the Good Lord down to their own size. Scriptures address this. Remember the workmen who went early into the field to work for a coin? Others, I don't recall just how many, didn't get to work until later, others arrived just before quitting time. Each group was promised a coin. At quitting time each man got his coin. Those who came early wanted those coming late penalized, but the farmer told them to be satisfied, they'd agreed to their wages. The late comers were to get full pay because he, the farmer, said so. End of debate."

W. H. went on expounding on the pride of those who questioned the farmer, thinking their judgement better than his. "These people who doubt that Grifton got salvation during those last days are like those early workers, trying to usurp the authority of the property owner, their pride raising them to the level of the Lord. Won't do, Caleb!"

W. H., his arm outstretched, his hand opened wide, made a wide sweep, as if to say this is for the whole world. In his deepest base voice, he said, "Mr. Grant, it will not do to listen to a man who knows only his religion. Note, I said, his religion—emphasis on his. Nor will it do to listen to the man who knows only economics or only liberal arts. Mix it up a little, like Jefferson and De Vinci, not that I totally agreed with either." He gave me that look again as if to say, you got that didn't you.

"It's fine to go into the woods for inspiration as the great writer Thoreau did. But one must get out into the open fields, the streets, the factories, the government offices, the homes to make application." At this W. H. leaned forward, nodded, and sat back looking very satisfied with himself.

"Well, I see why people doubt Grifton's regeneration. Life in his lane was lurid. The rumors and the supported facts about Grifton were there. They're still commanding, or at least competing for dominance in my mind," I said, my frustration obvious.

"True, true, Caleb, but let us examine this. Recollect the great King David? Hard to find a more lurid life than his—the underbelly of man one might say, clearly exposed right there in the Holy Scriptures. Lust, adultery, murder: lurid, now I submit these acts were lurid. Yet, it is written that he was a man after the Lord's own heart. How can that be?" I knew W. H. wasn't waiting for me to explain, so I just shook my head and said nothing, but did think about Grifton's contributions to the needy children.

W. H. ran his hand along the crown-crease in his hat, looked across the lawn toward the jail, and proceeded.

"You see, one must read the rest of the report to understand David's true nature, which no doubt resulted in his granted position. Read the Psalms. There we find a contrite heart, a heart crying out to the Lord, asking for forgiveness, protection, acknowledging the role of the great Creator, his omnipotence, omnipresence." W. H. wasn't acting like an evangelist, wasn't trumpeting, or hacking, but his reasoning sounded much like one.

He stormed on, not loud, but stormy, excited. "Without the Psalms you do not see David, the real man. Scriptures go on to say, in so many words, that we, the redeemed, are still just like David—spiritual men, natural men. Natural men are subject to do most anything, good or bad." W. H. lowered his head and looked at me from under his eyebrows.

"What about Christ?" I was still considering the indigenous Americans and their relationship.

"Caleb, this is just my interpretation you understand, but if we accept that God is love, what more expression of that love can possibly be exposed than Christ himself. No man ever has or ever will walk the earth to show us The Father as Christ did. Follow Him—eliminate anger, hate, murder, war, lust, stealing, coveting, guile, haughtiness. Pure hearts emerge, humble spirits, merciful spirits, peacemaking spirits, witnessing spirits." W. H. crossed his arms, resting them on his huge midsection.

I looked at him and thought: knock a few rough edges off and he'd make a passable preacher. Even Fred, the old deacon, might agree.

I removed what looked to be a discarded orange seed from the bench seat and flipped it into the dirt at my feet. "So, you think the Americans before the Europeans got here were not saved?" I asked.

"No, no, not by any means." W. H. thrust his hands before him palms up, I thought somewhat exasperated with my denseness.

"The Lord makes that decision, not me. Abraham, the old patriarch, you know, was traipsing around in a dark land, but not in the dark. His faith saved him; no scriptures available so far as we know." W. H. took a deep breath, scratched under his shirt collar. He seemed to be evaluating what he'd just said. "Yes, I know, scripture says we must believe in Christ, his God-man makeup, and it asks the question: how can men believe unless they hear? But It's not my place to judge those who have never heard this. The Lord will take care of those people wherever they are in his own way."

The sun had gone down, the streets now empty. A young man leaned against a no-parking sign at the curb as W. H. and I got up to make our way to our respective homes. W. H. took my arm as we were about to part. "Hellfire, Caleb, these gossips, judges of mankind can't determine Davis's salvation, just as you and I can't. True repentance and faith determine that; baptism in a wash pan? That's symbolic, just as it would be if conducted in the lake behind your house." W. H. squared his shoulders, tugged at his tie, and waddled off.

It suddenly dawned on me, Mandy is not going to be happy. Supper time has passed. I've been gone since breakfast. I'll just have to weigh the *bad eye* treatment against getting to spend a couple of hours sitting on a hard bench in front of the court house listening to a slightly vulgar-talking theologian, counselor, blow-heart, friend.

UNEXPECTED QUEST

I was out before breakfast, thankful for the time alone to enjoy the great creation. A fog hung heavy over the horse pasture, dew wet my shoes, threatening my socks. The sun was somewhere up there but not yet visible. JD, the horse, was at the far gate away from the barn. I couldn't see him for the fog, but heard his neigh when I called his name, then his steady foot-falls as he paced to where I stood with the salt. On these occasions I always remove my hat and leaning forward over the fence await his greeting. He nuzzles my forehead and unless I step back extends his long slick tongue and licks, leaving slobber to the hairline. JD's salt appropriately delivered, I returned to the barn, re-stacked the drying lumber, adjusted the right-hand lever on the lawnmower, and spent considerable time searching for pliers on the workbench. Giving up on finding the pliers, and having forgotten why I was looking for them, I stepped out on the porch. The fog had lifted, or whatever happens to fog. Anyway, the sun was shining, reflecting brightly off the wet grass and JD's coat. Raising my eyes to look side to side, then far over the pasture, I chuckled, thinking of Mandy's dad's comment fifty some years earlier—to look high and wide as you go out each morning.
A robin hopped and pecked, hopped and pecked perilously close to JD's hoof, Mandy's cat, Yellow Tom, squatted twenty or so yards away wagging his tail menacingly, and looking at a grey squirrel running along the top board of the fence. The review over, I checked the time. While glancing at the watch, the notion struck me that something was not right. The surrounding mental-picture was somehow incomplete. The next viewing again included the bird, the horse, the cat, the far fence, and the lake. That's it!
The boat was gone. No sign of it. Unlikely, but possible that the tie came loose or broke, it slipped the anchor and drifted. But where? Just to be certain I walked over to the

water's edge, walked the bank for a hundred or so feet focusing, looking hard into the water—no sign of a sunken boat, no sign of an anchor, no sign of the tie ropes. The logical alternative: drive to the marina, report the lost boat, and request help. I yelled in to Mandy, as I passed the screened in porch where she was watering flowers and fern, "Hold breakfast, please. I'll be back shortly." She grunted something back.

The marina operator was concerned and helpful. He notified boaters on the lake who had radios to watch for the boat. He requested the local airport dispatch officer to send a small plane up. A hundred miles of shoreline presented a substantial search area. The possibility that a boat of that size could drift far without someone noticing was improbable. It was late afternoon before the marina report was complete. Neither the boaters or the flight pilot had anything to report. Mr. Satterley, the marina owner, reluctantly offered, "Caleb, is it possible someone borrowed it"? I knew what he meant. The boat had not been boarded, at least by me, for over a week. I couldn't remember when I last noticed it.

Law enforcement was notified, and they began their inquiry after interrogating me. I say interrogate because that's what it felt like. Maybe they were ruling out an insurance fraud, or some such. The lake is an impoundment of the Cumberland River which flows west to Nashville and Paducah where it joins the Ohio. Upriver the Cumberland penetrates deep into Eastern Kentucky. In total it travels nearly seven hundred miles. If the boat is not on the lake, then where? My mind was scooting over these miles seeing the river in Harlan County, a mere trickle compared to Cumberland County in south central Kentucky where it spreads wide and flows leisurely toward Nashville. Meanwhile an unlikely scene was playing out. Ace and Duce were leaning back in deck chairs, rising now and then to toss a beer can overboard, open another, or light up.

"That asshole overcharged us for diesel back there." They had passed through the Wolf Creek Dam and were making their way toward Nashville. "I know what it costs, saw it on the Shell sign down from the house many a time." Duce, using what was left of his disability back pay, was financing the adventure. Not realizing how much fuel a boat of that size used, the size of the tanks, and the excessive cost at marinas Duce was upset.

"Cost of doing business," Ace was loose. It wasn't his money and the special smoke was working its miracle. During one of their highs the men had concocted a plan. "Beat the cost of getting high," Ace had explained. "Go to the source, make a little cash: Steal Pop's boat. Float down to St. Louis or New Orleans, pick up a load of drugs and bring them back to Kentucky, sell them retail."

But, as they floated gently to the marina near the next dam, business went sour. Ace and Duce had failed to calculate the cost of fuel. Their money was short some forty dollars, and they tried to trade one of the bedroom TV's for the balance. The attendant filling the tanks declined their offer but agreed to grant some time while they walked into town carrying the flat screen; "a deal," was to be made, according to Ace. Things went downhill from there. A pawnbroker finally agreed to pay fifty dollars for the TV, and the men exited his establishment in somewhat of a strut.

In the parking lot adjacent to the pawn shop, the two encountered three kindred spirits. "Hey, dudes," the tall one said. "Come over here and experience your wildest ride yet."

The tall man, wearing a cowboy hat, referred to himself as Wrangler. An unlikely name, Ace thought. Probably never sat a saddle. His greasy hair strung from under his hat in matted strands. Instead of boots, he wore running shoes, the sole flapping on one. A pirate tattoo was prominently visible on his left forearm. His dark eyes shifted constantly side to side—definitely no cowboy wrangler. The other two in dungarees, worn dangerously close to indecent exposure and dirty tee shirts, grinned like stage puppets waiting for their controller to lend them voice.

Ace and Duce, now running low on pills and smokes joined the crew—bohos always ready to join those of like stripe. In an alley just off the Main Street, needles shared, eyes, mind, and body dulled to reality, Ace and Duce bragged about their bold plan, their long trip, but revealed their shortage of cash. The wrangler and his two compatriots, all three unanchored, readily joined in a partnership to finance the trip for a share of profits and the five were soon on their way south, luxuriously riding the great river. Wrangler had to assume responsibility for handling the boat as Ace and Duce sprawled snoring on the deck. Wrangler motioned for his two puppets to come close.

"These two losers are amateurs." Wrangler gestured toward Ace and Duce. "We don't need to share squat with them." So, the three agreed to Wrangler's plan to put Ace and Duce ashore at the next convenient spot.

As the sun dropped low in the west, a great eagle screamed overhead, a huge big-mouth bass jumped high out of the water. Duce, waking up ahead of Ace, yelled at Wrangler, "Heh, what the shit are you doing so close to the bank? Want to ground us?" Ace and Duce both sunbaked were on their feet moving toward Wrangler, but the puppets intervened. Ace and Duce were thrown overboard near a rotting dock, built years ago by some local property owner for his private use. Sputtering and spewing, the two hung on to the anchor post of the old dock and watched what they liked to think of as their Dad's boat churn its way southwest toward Barkley Dam.

Just as well. As Ace and Duce made their way to a rural country store on a county road somewhere in Western Kentucky, Wrangler and his puppet friends were headed for an unwelcome rendezvous near Barkley Dam. Pictures of the boat along with notification of its being stolen had been forwarded to marinas east and west along the Cumberland. The next refueling sunk the Wrangler gang's hope of reaching a southern drug connection. The three were cuffed and hauled away to be charged with being in possession of stolen property, having illegal drugs on board, and being under the influence of drugs while operating a boat. Chuckling and looking at his tattoo, Wrangler said, "Guess we both let the other one down this time old buddy". The puppets stood grinning, ready to talk if given voice. Meanwhile, Ace and Duce were apprehended near the country store while attempting to hitch a ride back east. Wrangler told all. He and the puppets had pirated (his word) the boat from the Davises. The Davis men had first claimed that they were the owners, later changed their story to claim it belonged to their Dad. While clinging to the old pier post they had yelled that the boat belonged to a fellow in Kentucky, Caleb Grant, and that the Wrangler gang would be sorry they ever took it.

THE BOAT RECLAIMED

The State Police called me about ten p.m. to report having retrieved my boat somewhere in the neighborhood of Barkley Dam in far Western, Kentucky. "Headed, for the Ohio, or maybe the Mississippi," the officer reported. Three men were arrested. A third man surprised me. Only Ace and Duce had shown up on the marina tapes. The officer directed me to come to Grand Rivers, Kentucky in Livingston County, "Bring the boat title and claim your property," he said.

I faced a day's drive with two assistants, one to help with the boat, the other to get my car back home not to mention other expenditures I'd just as soon not make—fuel costs, and un-telling what boat repairs and clean-up faced me.

"What about Ace and Duce?" I asked.

The officer laughed. "Oh, they weren't on the boat."

"What do you mean, 'they weren't on the boat?'" Was he not talking about my boat?

The officer cleared his throat and resumed quickly to allay the fear reflected in my voice. "Ace and Duce were located several miles away, after we halted the boat and interrogated the three passengers." The officer paused and sort of apologized. "My laughing was inappropriate, I'm sorry, but this has been the dangest situation," he said, then laughed again. I failed to see any humor.

"Mr. Grant, your local men stole the boat, picked up three, shall we say hitchhikers, who threw your rouges overboard and pirated the boat." Again, the officer laughed, "one of the high jackers has a prominent pirate tattoo on his forearm."

After reclaiming the boat, I spent the better part of the next week cleaning, replacing the TV and sections of carpet. Had troublesome thoughts about Ace and Duce, too— actually wanted to slap them around a little. Of course, with the age and strength difference that was out of the question.

As to the five pirates, I don't have a lot of information as to what happened with the courts. The officers took my statement about Wrangler and the two puppets, and I heard no more. Ace and Duce's case was transferred to our home county. W. H. wound up as their representative and called me a month or so later.

"Hello, Captain." W. H. was in a jovial mood. "Guess you heard I got your men's case assigned to me. Stole your boat, headed to the Gulf. Hellfire, Caleb! What's this world coming to? Reverted back to the nineteenth century, if you ask me. Sounds like Tom Sawyer and Huck Finn. What do you want me to do? This can go hard on those parasites, or I can likely get their charges reduced, save the county some money."

Time had softened my thoughts considerably. "W. H., give me the alternatives, if you will," I said.

"If you push this, Caleb, and I work my trade, these men might still get several years. They don't have much leverage with the court, considering their past. On the other hand, if you don't press charges, they could be released right soon. Unlike King Richard of old, if my memory serves me correctly, people aren't lining up to raise ransom in behalf of these two scoundrels."

I asked W. H. what he thought I should do. "Hellfire, Caleb, send them up and save the streets. Turn 'em loose and save the county. You lose either way." I asked W. H. to let me think about it a few days.

Mandy and I had a right serious discussion after W. H.'s call. "Send them away," Mandy said. "Make the streets a little safer". I heartily agreed. Next morning at breakfast we resumed the conversation. A night to sleep on the matter and I grew softer. After all, the boat had belonged to their Dad. I had allowed them to spend time on it. My Grifton study had brought them into our circuit. I was conflicted. Mandy, after hearing my concerns, softened too.

"There is a chance for redemption. No one was hurt. I've heard terrible stories about prison, you know, how incarceration with society's worst just hardens such men as Ace and Duce," she said.

After the morning discussion with Mandy, I contacted W. H. and reported no charges were to be pressed against the Davises on my part.

"Hellfire, Caleb, you're too good for your own good." W. H.'s pronouncement wasn't given in a condemning way even though he expressed it with the expletive introduction. A couple of months went by. The Grifton pursuit languished. I piddled around the place. On a Saturday about mid-day, while engrossed with JD's grooming, I was interrupted, startled actually, by two men who had stealthily walked up behind me. One placed his hand on JD's rump.

"Hey, Mr. Grant," a big smile spread across Ace's face.

"Thought we'd come by and see you," Duce said.

"Yeah and apologize to you and thank you for being so good to us." Ace chimed in.

They soon got down to business. "We found a note," Duce said. Their story unfolded. The two had been searching the boat for money to pay for fuel and had stumbled onto something. Removing a picture hanging over the master bed, thinking a safe or something might be concealed there, they had noticed an imperfection in the sheet rock. The remainder of the boat had paneling, but the section behind the headboard was different. The indentation might have been a patch over something of value. They cut it away and found nothing but a crude drawing with hardly readable writing under a crudely drawn square. "Thought you might like to look at it." Duce rubbed his head.

I had never looked behind the huge picture, too large for the room, I always thought. It portrayed a beautiful, but fierce, black stallion, reared on its hind feet, pawing the air, nostrils flared, mane flying, and teeth bared. Pretty serious picture hanging over one's head at night. A Grifton message to all comers, or maybe a turn-on for his women friends. I examined the map but couldn't make much sense of it. However, the scribbling gave a hint. The square was marked with north, south, east, west labeled. Written near the bottom, "old Houston's place." An arrow pointed northwest and the number printed on the shaft indicated three hundred yards. The arrow point stopped in the middle of a circle. From discussions with Ulysses "Knot Head" Turner, I had a good idea what I was looking at.

I thanked the men and immediately wondered why I should be thanking the rogues, then dismissed them by saying that I'd look the find over and get with them later. I didn't know whether to call FBI agent Bunch, since this could possibly be Grifton's money safe, or search first.

That night I slept little. Scenarios plagued my mind as to what to tell the Davis men. I was tired of the quest, fed up with the two and wanted loose from the entire mess. First, I thought through one report suitable to W. H.'s recommendation, then one that Mandy and I might concoct, and third, one that seemed more appropriate to me. The next morning, I put the ideas to paper in draft form.

W. H.'S RECOMMENDATION:

Dear Robert and Bedford:

The last time I talked with your Dad he made a request that I tell you about him. Following is a report of what I know:

*He built good houses and a wonderful houseboat

*He gambled, set up an illegal insurance scam, got caught and served time.

Caleb

Those two sentences fulfilled W. H's. recommendation. I read them over but felt no satisfaction. This had been several years work. How could it be summed up in so few words?

FROM DICUSSIONS WITH MANDY:

Dear Robert and Bedford:
For some time now, I have been working on a project for
your Dad. The last time we talked, it was down at the
Chevron Station, he made a request. He asked that I tell
you two about him. He showed pictures of you when you
were ten or so years old, good looking boys, I might add.
That last meeting was after he had served time in prison,
prior to his bout with cancer, and before your school-
burning trouble. I agreed, and this is my final report to you.
You may wonder why so late. You needed to mature. I
needed to find you. It has taken years to put together
something to do justice to the family. These may just be
excuses, given because I have no concrete answer.
You might also question why I felt obligated to follow
through on such an odd request. Actually, I wonder too.
The answer is history, I suppose. Your Dad and I go back
more than sixty years. We were never close friends exactly,
didn't travel in the same circles, but respected one another
in our own way. He supported me in politics. I bought his
boat. He had a very charming way about him, always
friendly, upbeat, and encouraging at least toward me.
He was very proud of you two. So, this report is meant to
be respectful, truthful, and comprehensive to the extent of
my capabilities.
Grifton was a man of many talents. He grew up in a hollow
without the modern amenities that we take for granted—
indoor plumbing, electricity, a road to the outside world.
His education was extremely limited, attending school only
three years. His father, Happy, worked him like a man
when only a boy, taught him to gamble, revealed to him a
deceiving con-man personality, worked the log woods, and
farmed some. His mother struggled, working long days
seven days a week, building fires, milking, gardening,
preserving food, washing clothes in a huge tub outside in

summer, in the cellar in winter, ironed with a flat iron heated on the cook stove or in the fire place. The picture is clear. Grifton had a rough start.

Leaving home at fifteen, he developed into manhood on his own, loading coal, hustling work where he found it, with little or no adult direction. He no doubt saw many things unsuitable for a fifteen-year-old boy. Maturing under these circumstance, that is, living by his wits, forming habits, a world view was solidified that was legally unacceptable. At the same time, he developed exceptionable survival skills— paying mortgages on new trucks far ahead of schedule, profitably hauling coal and watermelons, selling cutlery, trading in jewels and antiques.

Supplementing these business activities and hard work, he followed the dice and card tables across the state and nation. He recruited and trained a cadre of family and acquaintances to cheat the insurance companies. These things I substantiated in my research.

Following are rumors that flowed like a foul wind throughout the community. Remember, these are unsubstantiated rumors and are reported as such. I questioned whether to include them, but finally concluded that you had already heard them and might take them to be facts:

*He cheated at cards and dice.
*He obtained jewels under questionable circumstances.
*He trafficked in drugs.
*He was somehow involved in his wife' murder.
*He kept an unwholesome household for children.
*He received no religious training, nor provided any.

These rumors are passed around and many times laughed about, but they are no laughing matter. It is my prayer that you will study this report, take the positives as personally worthwhile and achievable. Discard the rumors as just that, and stay away from all that is unjust, illegal, dangerous, and doomed.

Don't hesitate to call on me if further explanation is needed or if you just need to talk about any of the issues.
Otherwise, I will not be contacting you again.
Caleb Grant

PERSONAL THOUGHTS FOR THE DAVIS REPORT

Dear Robert and Bedford:

How we begin the race, how we run it, and how we end it are all important. Your Dad, when you were just boys made a request of me. "Grant," he said, "I want you to tell my boys about me." He smiled and showed your pictures. I bragged on the pictures and considered the strange request. You had different mothers, lived in different houses, had grown through early childhood in his absence. It began to make at least some sense. Your knowledge of him was probably limited. You likely heard rumors.

Some of what I'm going to report will be hard to swallow. That's why I began by talking about the race. This race represents how we proceed through life. As my friend, Fred Winkler, the old deacon, likes to expound, the great Apostle wrote about the race in the holy scriptures. He encouraged us to keep running, don't give up, that while the entire race is important, the end is weighted heaver. In other words, win. Win against yourself, against your, "Me first", nature.

Your Dad began the race with a terrible handicap. He had little wholesome home life, virtually no education, a life on his own during his formative years, and in bad company much of his adult life. I witnessed to him about Jesus, and salvation, but was rebuffed, "it's too late for me," he always said.

Well, I have some good news. It wasn't too late. When Grifton lay sick, he called for the preacher, repented, was baptized, and accepted the salvation available to all. You may hear talk about deathbed repentance, how it is useless. That is for the Lord to decide. Pay no attention. A man hanging on the cross beside Jesus, as both were dying, repented and the Lord assured him of a place in heaven. Now I present this first to give you encouragement or hope. The remainder of the report provides little of either.

Grifton was not a good man. He cut corners in life producing poor fruit. He and members of your family spent time in prison, paying for those short-cuts. Greed ruled. Many suffered. You are familiar with circumstances that brought about their incarceration. One can place blame on nurture. His upbringing was atrocious in the eyes of most. Personality is shaped by early interactions. Law, and natural law play a part. There is no pass, however, for wrong behavior. In other words, taking from others to satisfy personal desires, and leaving those others to replenish as best they can is unacceptable in society. Your taking my boat, for example: I didn't push the issue. You two got a partial pass, as you have on several occasions. This may sound like I'm preaching to you, and I guess I am, but it is my earnest desire that you find that "click" which releases awareness, that "curb" that holds back those self-serving actions that lead to trouble.

Seek alternative behaviors, behaviors that come from helping, serving others, versus the all for me attitude prevalent in so many of your actions. First thing is to stay away from the drugs that dull discernment in decision making. You have been involved in the drug culture long enough that stepping away on your own is highly unlikely. Long term rehabilitation including counseling, interpersonal relationships training, general education, and vocational schooling—a must. Learning how to live in a new environment may be the most difficult and the most important. Learning to avoid the Wrangler personalities. Living and working some place where you are less likely to encounter these addicts, these society drop-outs will be difficult. Live among those who establish and carry out productive goals. Finally, follow-up in NA or AA on a scheduled basis. Your race after drugs will be hard for a lifetime but associating with people successfully running the same track is another must.

These new behaviors, new thought patterns, new desires relative to lifestyle cannot be instilled in you by others. They must come forth from within. They must be struggled for, exercised daily if the transition is to be made. I'll be glad to discuss these issues with you, to put you in touch with professionals who specialize in these things. Ace, Duce, it's a matter of life and death. Look around you. Consider the large numbers, your sister Georgia Bell, being one of thousands—victims of early death.

You watched your mothers suffer as a consequence of their involvement with Grifton, their poor relationship with the community. You observed their lonely, hopeless lives lived essentially as single mothers; mothers who had no special training, no inheritance, and few of this world's comforts. They lived in a trench covered over with a dense cloud. Products of trench-living families see nothing ahead but the trench and the lessons learned there. These lessons are passed from parent to offspring. Turn to the side, look out over the trench beyond your surroundings, your training and habits. Climb out, rise up above the cloud. Break the cycle.

Enough preaching, lecturing, I want to get back to your Dad. He had some good traits; moving out of county to insure advanced training for your half-sister; giving money to support children's issues; feeding, clothing the family. He was thinking about you fellows the day he made the request of me. What he wanted me to say, I can't be sure; to tell you his experiences, how they led downhill in so many ways? Tell you about another way? That's what this letter turns out to be. Hopefully, it meets his approval.
Caleb

I went to bed after making this first stab at producing the Grifton report; unsettled as to which version to present but pleased that the end of the assignment was in sight. Even so, something still nagged me.

ULYSSES ASSISTS

The Davises' discovery of the paper in the wall of the boat still intrigued and troubled me. Obviously, it was left by Grifton. In discussion with Mandy, we concluded that involving the FBI was unnecessary since no law seemed to prevent me from exploring. If money were found, that was another matter. The name Houston was the only lead as to what the message was about, and Knot Head was the one who introduced me to that name. So, I contacted Knot Head, and he invited me to meet him at the McDonalds the following Saturday morning. No mention was made of the paper as I didn't want Knot Head to spread the word before further investigation. The woods full of treasure hunters was not a pleasant thought.

When I joined the coffee group on the appointed Saturday, W. H. was in a deep discussion. I heard him say, "*The World Is Flat*". I first thought the old counselor had hung around the jail house crowd too long or maybe Knot Head and his buddies.

W. H. went on to say, "You see, men, before Columbus sailed that mighty ocean, faced unheard of monsters, the many frequently discussed sea dangers, general consensus was that the earth was flat. You walk out or sail out there so far and you'd fall off into nothingness, fall somewhere into the ether itself. Now there is some argument as to how much navigational experts really knew at the time. Current theory is that Columbus knew better, that the world was actually round". W. H. coughed, clearing his throat, stirred in his coffee cup, took a noisy drink, wiped his mouth, and continued. "Be all that as it may, just proving the roundness of the earth by his journey flattened it."

Amos Moon jumped in. "I don't see how you can say that, W. H. Seems to me it just proved it was round." There were nods all around. W. H. was way out there this morning.

"Hold on Amos," W. H. said. "I'm about to reveal something to you."

By this time, I caught on that W. H. was quoting and paraphrasing a book by Thomas L. Friedman with the group. He looked around to be sure of their attention and resumed. "Over the years with steam power and other advances, this travel from Spain to the New World and later to Japan and China, allowed communication over long distances.

"Now, this is the hook, men, modern man can now deal in real time around the globe using electronic communications, internet, telecommunications. Say, I call my legal assistant, for instance, in Bangalore, India, ask for research on a case of import at five p.m. today, go home and get a good night's sleep. She works during her daylight hours. It's light over there when it's dark here, you know."

Knot Head was suddenly leaning far over the table, his Adams apple jiggling. "Yeah, I saw something on TV about that. You really got a workhand overseas?"

W. H. waved him off. "I arrive at the office the following morning, open the computer, and bam! There it is, a full report." W. H. looked around the table. Comprehension with this crew might require other examples.

"There what is?" Fred was scratching his head, looking from W. H. to the men around the table, trying to figure out if anybody understood.

"Why, my research report on the legal issue!" W. H. put considerable wind behind this response to be sure everybody got it.

Amos Moon was still hung up on the roundness of the earth. "W. H., it's a matter of geography. Any globe I look at is round. I turn it, find California, China, France, New York. This big outfit we're riding on is spinning, traveling. It's round."

"Granted, but Amos, don't you see, we've overcome the roundness. We've defied spinning. Time zones no longer separate us. Why, some of these restaurants just like we're sitting in right here are wired so that you place an order out there at the drive-in window and it doesn't come inside this building but goes some nine hundred miles away to a call center—in another time zone. Buttons are pushed there. You get your order handed out the window right here in this building."

"You mean I don't get to talk to Emily, the lady who asks if I want 'taters' with my order?" Amos was shaking his head.

They had heard enough. The men stood, pushing their chairs back, offering excuses for having to leave, glancing at one another, disappointment obvious on each face; their stories, had gone unstated, unheard. W. H. looked at me, lowered his head as if to say, "Oh, well, what can you expect? Ignorance runs deep".

W. H. grunted and pulled himself up. "I've got a very important case coming up Monday. I better be going too boys. Good to see both of you." He nodded at Knot Head, then me and left the table. I was somewhat interested in his discourse, but business with Knot Head was pressing.

"Knot Head," I said, "I need your expertise."

Knot head leaned far over the table, his cap bill nearly covering his eyes. "Sure 'nough?" His face lighting to think that someone had need of his expertise, but questioning also what he might offer, wood-cutting, tree trimming, road work, all went through his mind. "I'll be glad to help if I can," he said.

"You remember our discussion about Grifton Davis' boyhood, about your Uncle Houston?"

"Sure do. They's neighbors."

"I need you to go down in the hollow with me and show me where Houston lived."

"Ain't nothing there 'cept a briar patch now, a few old apple trees, but I'll be glad to go with you." Knot Head leaned back in his chair and crossed his arms over his chest, looking pleased to be asked.

"Can you do it this coming Monday?" I asked. We agreed to make the trip, but Knot Head needed to wait until after the mail run. He was expecting his electric bill and wanted to get the check in the box. Knowing that he had twenty or so days grace, I started to protest, but thought better of it. We decided I'd pick him up at nine.

The trip to Happy, Houston, and Grifton's hollow turned out to be more of a trip than anticipated. In miles, it's not that far, but travel route and time defy its proximity. Knot Head and I loaded up with bottled water, sandwiches, and dressed in tough outdoor clothing, and boots before leaving. Turns out all were needed. We traveled a state highway for a couple miles, turned on to a winding blacktop county road for a few miles, then to a county gravel road for several miles, and from that to a hard to follow overgrown pass-through (an unimproved road from yesteryear no longer in use). We drove through two branches flowing to the nearby river. I think it was two branches; it could have been one winding around the hills. "That's it!" Knot Head was excited. I didn't see anything except a sloping field overgrown with horseweeds, briars and saplings. "See over there the old apple orchard, and there's a hump, the old cellar. Finally catching up with Knot Head's visual, I saw both the orchard, two leaning trees, and the cellar, just a rolling hump in the earth from our perspective.

I stopped the truck and we made our way to the cellar. Nearby were the remains of a chimney, stones lying in various positions of rest, red from now cold fires. I looked at the paper.

"What's that you got, Caleb?" Knot Head inquired, straining his neck to get a look. I told him that I wasn't sure but thought it to be a marker map where something may be hidden. "You don't say." Knot Head's eyes were wide. He licked his lips and tugged at his coat collar. "What do you think it is?" I told Him that I had no idea but that he and I were going to find out. "Douse me," he said.

I centered myself in front of where the house likely stood, opened my phone measurement app, sighted what I thought to be the circle location and began walking. Knot Head was bouncing over briars, decaying tree limbs blown from the nearby woods by earlier storms. We passed an old dump site. Lead Mason jar lids, unmarked tin cans, likely local cannery relics from the days when garden produce was canned by locals at a central location—a product of the WPA period. A number two washtub lay mangled, the bottom rusted out, several bullet holes in what was left of the must-have family utensil.

We made our way the requisite three hundred yards only to be faced with a steep incline, no sign of a cave or whatever the circle represented. To our left, the hill fell away to a slope which revealed nothing. Right of us a drain curved steeply west carrying water away from the house site.

There was a small trickle of water running down the drain. "Wait a minute, Caleb. There used to be a right smart of a spring just up a little-ways, come right out of the hill." I acknowledged with a nod and we made the few feet climb. There it was, a rusting pipe carrying the water to pool at the head of the drain.

Not a storage place; heavy rains send gushing streams through these openings. The local karst landscape is laced with caves, holes where the limestone has weathered away allowing the water to seek its level. Oftentimes a stream will create one such path, then over the years eat its way through a layer and sink to a new path. A cave above a spring, that's it, I thought. Knot Head and I moved a few feet higher on the hill.

"Look here, Caleb." Knot Head in his enthusiasm had moved a few steps ahead. Sure enough, before us was an opening maybe three feet high and about the same width.

Now, what to do? Adrenalin took charge. Any tiredness dissipated, to be replaced with concern, fear actually. I dreaded sticking my head in that hole. I dreaded snakes, bats, spiders, a rock fall.

Knot Head, acting more like Ulysses, brought me out of the panic. "I'll go in, Caleb, I'm littler than you." With that he began scampering into the hole. "What am I looking for, Caleb?"

"Anything that looks out of place, not naturally found in such a place, anything manmade," I answered.

"Okay." He yelled.

I heard him scratching in the dirt. The opening closed off to a large crack after about ten feet in. "Ain't nothing buried here, best I can tell, and nothing on the surface out of ordinary, that I can see." Knot Head backed out of the cave. We both sat on a boulder, opened my back pack and ate and drank. Both had sunk in spirit. Silence surrounded us, except a family of crows settled down next to the old house site, apparently to have a family discussion.

I sat staring at a beetle, considering whether it expels a gas out its rear that causes a frog to vomit it back up. I had recently read about such a bug. Knot Head sat facing the old house site, likely seeing uncle Houston sitting on the back porch next to the well bucket, picking his banjo as the mist lifted from the hollow. No doubt both of us looked dejected, worn, and disappointed.

As the food and water began to replenish and refresh, thoughts moved on from the beetle. Knot Head risked himself going into that hole. I'm no scaredy-cat. There must be something in there. Grifton was certain I'd find the map note. I'm going in. I stood quickly, startling Knot Head out of his trance.

"What's the matter, Caleb?"

I answered, "nothing," and told him to come on. When we got to the cave, Knot Head took my arm.

"You ain't going in there are you? It's a waste of time. You might get snake bit or something." There it is, the greatest dread of my life when out enjoying the wilds.

"No, I won't," I said, and began the crawl. Once inside, the opening allowed me to stand almost erect, to examine the walls and ceiling. On my right very near the roof about five feet into the cave, a crevice maybe four inches wide stretched toward the back. I could reach it easily but was deathly afraid to put my hand in it. I called to Knot Head to toss me a stick.

"You ain't into it with something are ye?" he asked.

I told him, no, and picked up the stick he threw in, used it to prowl the crevice which dropped some inches just beyond the entrance. Satisfied that no snakes were going to come rolling out, I began seriously prodding. The stick hung on something, not soft and not hard either. Mustering my courage and wishing I had leather gloves, I plunged my hand in beside the stick where I could feel the something. Removing the stick, I got hold of whatever it was and pulled hard. Little by little a plastic bag, the size of a kitchen waste bag emerged, mashed as flat at the contents allowed and tied several times around and end to end with twine.

"Find something, Caleb?" Knot Head, overcome with anticipation, had half his body inside the cavity. I asked him to back out so we could get to better light.

Once outside, we sat and cut and unraveled string. The bag was brittle from exposure, but I managed to slide my hand inside and begin removing the contents. A tightly rolled cotton rag that looked like it might have been part of a shirt at one time was wrapped in twine, crisscrossed several times to ensure keeping the hard, round shape; a small metal hook probably from a piece of some tool used in logging; a set of blueprints folded neatly inside a plastic baggie; two sets of dice and a deck of cards; a set of keys attached by ring to a Mack truck emblem; another baggie contained a picture of Grifton in prison garb with his prison number across the bottom, a napkin with a Las Vegas logo on it, a certificate declaring Grifton a chef from a Las Vegas restaurant, a small ruby; in a third baggie was a small New Testament Bible—given out by the Gideon's for witnessing.

Knot Head looked perplexed. "What in the world" is all he said. I'm not sure if I wanted to find a bag chock full of cash or diamonds, or some other riches, or if I was just as pleased with the find. Mandy and I must peruse this, parse the meaning of each item.

It was nearly dark when I got back to town and dropped Knot Head off at his home. I decided to drive out by Ace and Duce's house on the chance of catching them. Explaining to them why I had pursued the hunt without taking them along was troubling; fearing their reaction at the sight of a stash of cash in a dark hollow had prevented my inviting them. Knot Head being the only one who knew where to go made him a necessary companion. The four-wheel drive truck with the console between the seats, that was to be my answer. Four people were too many for the cab.

The Davises regarded me lazily when I got to their house. The question never came up as to me making the find without taking them along. The encounter generally went without incident. "Is that all you found?" Duce posed the question. I nodded, and the two took each object, turned it over and pitched it back on the kitchen table that had been cleared of motorcycle parts, McDonalds wrappings, pizza boxes, a full ash tray, various dishes crusted from other days. I thought Duce looked a little suspicious when he inquired about the find.

"Looks like Pop was about out of something to do," Ace said, and laughed as he flung the last item on the table—the New Testament.

I asked how the motorcycle repair was coming. "Not so hot." Duce grimaced and took out the makings a cigarette, completed the product, lit up and added, "I'm gonna get me a new pickup soon's I get the money." Ace rolled his eyes and plumped down in a ragged easy chair.

Considering the visit on the way home I decided that the articles meant nothing to the two men. They readily allowed me to re-package and keep the lot. It wasn't until I got home and examined them with Mandy that I noticed the ruby was gone. It probably had little value, but their stealing it irked me.

The articles kept running through my mind on the drive home: string tied ball—stickball; metal hook—timber work; truck keys—hauling peaches, coal; chef certificate—cooking, selling cutlery; dice and cards—gambling; prison picture—insurance scam; ruby—precious jewel sales; blue print—houses he built; New Testament—salvation?

PARSING THE FIND

I offered no thoughts on the cave find to Mandy, just spread it on the kitchen table after breakfast the next morning. Before looking at the items Mandy asked, "What makes you so sure Grifton hid the note map for you"?

"I've questioned that myself," I said. "Actually, I don't know. Maybe it was left for posterity, not me, for someone to find years later and ponder."

"Or possibly, left to claim some weird sense of immortality," she said, without a mystical look on her face. I was glad of that. "You clearly established that Grifton played the odds throughout his life. Maybe he was just playing the odds counting on your not liking the picture, removing it, finding the wall patch, the map—search and find."

Mandy looked at me for follow-up. I just said, "Maybe." She picked up each item, examined it carefully, laid it down, and without comment went on to the next. When she'd completed the examination and as I finished reading the morning news, and swallowed the last of my coffee, she looked at me, shook her head and giggled. "This is a history of Grifton. That scallywag wanted you to give his boys his entire life story."

"That is my conclusion exactly." With that I began a serious review of each article. I may just give them the full findings, including the three summaries. Let them dig a little, that is, if they read it at all.

GRIFTON RESURRECTED

ACE AND DUCE: Now and again we stumble on information not looked for but welcome just the same, even if we have no use for the information. That's certainly the case with the story I'm about to pass on to you. More than a year, I say year, actually years now seem but months, so I can't be sure just how much time had passed after completing work on the Davis project. Mandy and I were in Pigeon Forge, Tennessee, shopping, reading billboards, dining, people watching, and just driving around as day tourists do. Mandy noticed a comedy barn advertisement;

GRIFTON, 7:00 pm, and 9:30 pm
Country Style Dining, Regional Foods.

"Caleb," Mandy said, "look at that!" She pointed to the billboard.

Gripping the steering wheel, I blurted out, "What in the world"! I quickly moved into the turn lane. This had to be investigated. That name showing up on a billboard; what are the chances? Turned out the ticket window didn't open for three more hours, but a subscript indicated that ticket reservations were available at the tourist center several blocks away.

After reserving tickets for the second show, I inquired what the show was about, the star's name. "New fellow in town. Stand-up comedian, making quite a hit," the clerk was smiling. "Cute, too," she concluded and winked at Mandy. Mandy returned what I thought to be a dry, short smile.

We passed the time browsing store fronts; Gap, Reebok, the Chop House, Banana Republic, Jones of New York, Brooks Brothers, and settled in at Starbucks. I'm still trying to adjust to four-dollar coffee. My first coffee back in the day cost a nickel.

The theater was a large gaudy (Mandy's word) affair with dinner tables set around the stage. A tall, slender man mounted the stage by leaping from among the dining tables. A spot light focused on his move. He grabbed the microphone in passing and slid to a stop to a loud drum roll.

"Hi'dy-ho ladies and gentlemen! My name is Grifton! I'm from Kentucky—incognito!" He leaned far back placing his hands before his face as though hiding. "Tonight, I'm here to correct some misconceptions that have developed over the past couple years." This Grifton was wearing glossy long pointed shoes, tight black slacks, a red long sleeve slipover, a neatly trimmed mustache, huge sunglasses, a porkpie hat, gold chains, and matching rings. Definitely modern cool.

Grifton quickly transformed into character, not in looks, however. He was playing the role of immigrant, probably from south of the border—maybe not altogether politically correct.

"I tell you one thing: Mr. Pres, he like Griff." He did a little dance step. "He tole me so, right on TV. I L-O-V-E you, he say. Say he wants to send me back home? Bull! Who gonna fix yo roofs, deadhead yo flowers, carry yo icey tea? Who gonna pick yo tomatoes, dig yo potatoes, lay yo brick? Tell me that!" Grifton bent forward toward the audience, removed his sunglasses for a better view, smiled, then grimaced and shook his head side to side. At first, I decided that he had seen a rerun of an earlier comedy TV character, Jose Jimenez, but later dropped that idea and just wondered.

"My Pres ain't sending nobody back. That big wall, it gonna keep us here. Jest tell old Griff, how he thinking on sending me back? Who you think install that gold toilet? Who hung that big gold sign on his house? Yo sure didn't.

Who fix it so old Griff don't have to pay no tax? That right, no tax, double deduction, you unerstand. Say he lie?" Grifton put his hand behind his ear and leaned far over the stage as though getting the statement from the crowd. "He might stretch a story a little now and then. Make it ineresting. Say he ain't got nine billion? See that fifty-grand jacket that pretty first lady, the one he married to, wore? I betcha he got fifty billion give or take a few. He got golf courses worth that much."

Grifton bowed low placing both hands on the stage floor. Rising, he said, "Yo remember now, keep yo focus on the mainest thing. Behave yo-selves! Act like yo thinks yo sister do. As the pretty blond Jackie sang before I's born, 'What the World Needs Now is Love Sweet Love'.

The show lasted over an hour, focusing primarily on the President. I've given you a sampling. It ended to raucous applause. Grifton left the stage as he mounted it—leaping down among the tables. It was definitely our Ace, but certainly not the one I'd become acquainted with.

Mandy leaned close, "Amateur, I have no idea who he was trying to mimic," was all she said. I was inclined to agree, but remembering the old Ace, I refused to say so.

Then, attempting a little levity, I said, "maybe as aunt Ora once said about your cousin Claud when he came home from Ohio with a midwestern brogue, 'he was trying to be somebody he ain't, and can't'".

After waiting in line for the well-wishers to finish with Ace, we finally reached his table. To my surprise, he hurriedly rose from his chair and embraced me in a big bear hug, then reared back, and curled his upper lip. "Did you see my new tooth? Well, it's not new now, but new since you saw me." I complimented him on his tooth, how well he looked, and his performance. Once greetings were settled, Ace said, "let's go sommers and get a bite to eat." still somewhat in character, I thought.

At the *Apple Barn*, we settled in, eating muffins smeared in apple butter and drinking coffee. Ace, eager to bring us up-to-date began immediately. "Bet you didn't think I'd do it, did you?" Without waiting for a response, he moved on. "I went from our last meeting, the one when you gave us that preachy letter, checked myself into rehab the very next day. Duce went too but stayed only thirty days. I hung on, got a full nine-months-worth." Ace grinned first at Mandy, then me. "Heck, it was paid for by the state or somebody, anyway didn't cost me a penny until the last five months. They got me a piddling job and took part of my check." Eager to find out about Duce, I interrupted and asked what he was doing.

"Hold on," Ace said, "I'll get to Duce later." His monologue continued. "We had group in rehab two times a day." Ace frowned. "They called it therapy. I guess it was. It was dull though. After thirty or so days, I decided to perk it up a little. That's when I developed the routine you saw tonight. No matter what was being discussed, when I got the floor, I made them laugh. People say, laughing is good for you. I told the leader that, first time he tried to quieten me. He finally gave up and I took all the time I needed, getting the old deadheads to whoop and holler a little."

Ace excused himself, took out his phone and said, "hello, Robin Red. I'll be home late, late, having a snack with some old friends. I know. I promised you but understand these are friends of my Dad as well. No, I'm not going to get into anything, bye".

Ace looked at Mandy. "That was my accountability partner, my red-headed beauty, and roommate." Mandy nodded, but said nothing. "You inquired about Duce. Well, he didn't take to the rehab. Too much structure, I guess." Ace turned his head and upper body, popping something. "Duce fell in with one of the patients, a carnival worker. She looked like a dancer to me, know what I mean?" I didn't know for sure but nodded anyway. "Him and that dancer took off in the middle of the night, never told a soul."

Ace now had what I took to be a sly look. "I didn't hear a thing from Duce for over four months. Out of the clear, he called one night. I was still in rehab. He gave me the lowdown. Got a job as roust-a-bout for the carnival company, the one the dancer worked for, followed it all the way to Florida. The dancer kicked him out the first night in Sarasota for some infraction—drugs, I'm guessing." Using both hands, Duce drummed out some beat on the table. "Now, this next part you may have trouble believing. He went to work with a landscaping business. That was over a year ago. He's now supervising a crew of fifty, doing everything from trimming trees to laying sod. Would you ever have thought? Disabled to productive in a little over a year. Also, he's driving a new Dodge hemi, four-wheel drive!"

Mandy was not as impressed by Ace's report as I was. "I hope what we heard will last with those two. I'd like to see what Robin Red looks like," she said, as we drove toward home.

HOME AGAIN WITH AFTER THOUGHTS

I decide to write a run down on the McDonalds friends, that is, what little I know about them:

WILLIAM HARRISON, W. H., is still shuffling/waddling to the court house. One thing though: rumor is he's leading a Bible study group over at the Presbyterian Church and is committed to memorizing *Mac Beth*. He gets some criticism for not giving members of the group the floor to fully express their opinions. Also, he now seldom says "hellfire" down at the McDonalds. Gout still plagues him.

AMOS MOON is in the nursing home, temporarily, we hope; the result of an automobile accident. When his stay had to be extended past ninety days, he and his wife decided to divorce, something to do with Medicaid paying the bill. Thing is, she promptly married her childhood sweetheart. I visit often as possible. He needs to talk— usually a repeat of what he said on the previous visit.

KNOT HEAD has taken up gospel singing in local Pentecostal Churches. His witnessing trademark—'end times'. Elmer Sigmon questioned him at the Mc Donalds as to how he was doing, referring to income: "Oh," Knot Head said, "pretty fair. Course if there is somebody in the congregation up again it, say been bad sick, and if the preacher will vouch for them, we give the money to him or her." Knot Head now prefers to be addressed as Brother U. Turner. His friends at the McDonalds refer to him as Rev U. Turn—behind his back of course.

FRED WINKLER, fed up with First Baptist squabbles, has started a new church out on old US Highway 27, in a new metal building—white with a steeple on top. The sign out front says:

Not listed on the sign is the fact that Bobby Winkler is Fred's grandson. I also left off the saying of the day or week as it frequently changes.

ELMER SIGMON has been elected county magistrate from his district and now introduces himself as Squire Sigmon and expects others to so address him. His immediate goal is to implement a cat ordinance in the interest of his wife's flowers. Fat neighborhood cats of all colors and stripes stroll through Mrs. Sigmon's garden leaving behind their urine and lightly buried scat.

FORREST DAVIS has moved from the lake to a country estate trimmed in gold, so to speak. Apparently, the IRS and FBI aren't looking.

DEL, Peachy's brother, is still in California and doing well so far as I know.

GRIFTON, as you well know has gone on, but his story is now committed to print for posterity, progeny, and the shelf.

CALEB AND MANDY: We're managing. Mandy is doing her Goodwill shopping tours with sister Eunice, and DAR work with other qualified members. I'm listening down at the McDonalds and the court house, the post office, and on street corners for a newspaper expose`, or a report that needs to be written up for broader circulation.

PERSONAL CONCLUSION

Twenty-first century wisdom is likely to label the Griftons of this world as merely products of their times. I'm not that certain. Stumble into a cave thousands of years ago and count off a given population grouping. I'm guessing you'd find a Grifton, a product of mankind, not the times: his dice, and cards of a much different technology, none-the-less gaming devices; his diamonds and bangles, probably bone or stone, trade goods just the same; his irresponsibly spreading his seed just as common; his need to be liked, to be remembered harbored in his heart, and scratched on rock; the real self always guarded, hidden; finding life's shortcuts and taking them; fearing the end.

In other words, the Grifton personality, as a natural product of mankind, has likely been manifested throughout the ages. A number of today's local backpacker homeless previously discussed will have a Grifton, the local church likely has one, even big-time oligarchs have members exhibiting Grifton behavior—same as those cave men who hunkered in front of their hole in the ground, the cloud above and below always there—the Griftons always present.

THE END

NOTES:

1. The insurance scam and characters referenced in the book are fictional; however, the scam format is taken from a 1990's 6th District, U. S. Court case, and from 1990's newspaper accounts.

2. Fred Winkler's Church conflict discussions are fictionalized accounts based on internet writings from various parts of the country dealing with the Calvinist, Reformed movement in Baptist Churches. Also, the book *A Quiet Revolution* by Reisinger and Allen, while not quoted, played a role in formatting the discussions. Finally, articles from the internet on What Baptists Believe were reviewed and influenced the writing but not directly quoted.

3. The conclusions drawn about Peachy's childhood trauma and adult reaction to it are roughly based on the *Adverse Childhood Experiences Study (ACE)* done by the American Health Maintenance Org. Kaiser Permanente, and the CDC, 1990's.

ABOUT THE AUTHOR

Roland D. Mullins lives in Mt. Vernon, Rockcastle County, Kentucky. Now retired, his writing is strongly influenced by a lifetime of Appalachian living, serving as a teacher, school administrator, health care CEO, Mayor, County Judge executive, and farmer.

Email: mullinsrol@gmail.com

OTHER BOOKS BY ROLAND MULLINS
The Laurel Spur 2012
Aunt Beck 2016